A VITAL KILLING

AHMAD DEHGHAN

A Vital Killing
Translated from the Persian
By Caroline Croskery

Printed by CreateSpace, An Amazon.com
Company
CreateSpace, Charleston, SC

First Edition, 2015.
Printed by CreateSpace

eStore address:
https://www.createspace.com/5726528

Available from Amazon.com and other retail outlets
Available on Kindle and other devices

ISBN-13: 978-1517253967
ISBN-10: 1517253969
Printed in the United States of America

A Vital Killing
By Ahmad Dehghan

Translated by Caroline Croskery

Table of Contents

PASSENGER..6

QUAILS..16

A DOG'S LIFE 24

STAMPS 30

THE TICKET..46

THE MERMAID 56

A VITAL KILLING 66

THE RETURN 76

THE DEAD END 84

THE GIFT 94

ABOUT THE AUTHOR..108

ABOUT THE TRANSLATOR...110

In the Name of God

PASSENGER

I was leaving for work that morning when the postman stopped right in front of me on his rattletrap motorcycle. He took a look at the house number and then without saying a word, handed me an envelope addressed to me. I turned it over and saw Naneh Maryam's name and address on the other side.

I went quickly back inside the house and opened the letter. There were scribbles all over the faded paper, but in-between the crooked lines you could discern the faint shape of a person lying down with the covers pulled up to his chin. Laylee and I gradually discovered this together, meaning that I never left for work that day. I had gone back into the house and closed the door behind me. Laylee rolled out of bed and emerged from the bedroom and asked, "Have you forgotten something?"

I gave her the letter and said, "Look. It's from Naneh Maryam." She peered at me as she sleepily brushed aside her tousled hair – and suddenly realizing what I had said, she grabbed the letter and asked, "What are these scribbles?"

We then went into the bedroom and sat down next to each other on the edge of the bed and turned the paper every which way until we were able to discern the figure in the scribbles.

Someone else had certainly mailed it because Naneh Maryam didn't have the level of literacy needed to address the envelope. This worried me. I took off my coat and threw it on the bed. I walked into the den and called Jassem. He wasn't there, or at least no one answered. Laylee brought in the telephone book and we called a few more places from the phone numbers that we had, looking for Jassem – but we couldn't find him.

I didn't know what to do. Laylee felt just like I did. Having combed her hair and washed her face, she was now back by my side, staring at my lips waiting for me to say something. I was dumbfounded. Laylee said that it might make better sense to call Naneh Maryam's house and speak to her myself. I dialed her number and she picked up the phone. She said in her throaty, local accent, "Who is it?"

"Hello Naneh," I said, "it's me, Nasser."

"Are you calling from the front?" she asked.

I said, "No, Naneh, I'm not. This is Nasser, Abdo's friend. Do you remember me, Naneh?"

8

She said quietly and calmly, "Abdo is sleeping. He is tired." I could tell she didn't recognize me.

I repeated slowly, "Naneh Maryam, I am Nasser. I used to come to your house with Abdo when the war was going on. Do you remember me?"

At first she said nothing. Then without answering me, she continued what she was saying, "Haven't you heard? Abdo is back. My child was at war. Now he's back and is in his room sleeping. My child is very tired. But if you need to speak with him, I'll wake him up."

I said, "Naneh, do you remember when we came to your house. I'm the one you wrote to. I got your letter today. Do you remember me?"

She didn't say anything. I called her name a few times and thought maybe we were cut off. Then she said, "Oh, Abdo finally came back. I went myself and brought him back. I found him in the middle of the battlefield, my child."

I said, "Well, where is he now?"

She answered, "I said he is sleeping. They weren't going to let him come home. I knew he would come home on his own if he could. So I went to find him and bring him home myself."

Trying to make sense out of her irrelevant answers was draining me. I said, "Naneh, do you remember I came to your house in Ahwaz at the New Year with Laylee, my wife and my daughter, Negar? We came to the village and stayed the night?"

At first she didn't say anything, then she continued, "God-willing, I will find him a wife. There

9

are many nice girls in the tribe. Now will you have my Abdo as your husband?"

She was much worse off than the last time I had seen her.

I hung up. I called the office and told them I was not well and that I would be in a little later. Laylee was now worried and asked, "What did Naneh Maryam say?"

I said, "What can I say? She said Abdo has come back and is taking a nap."

She said, "When we went south for the New Year, didn't Jassem say that his mother was improving?"

She didn't wait for my answer and got up and went into the kitchen. I could hear her light the gas stove as I lay down on the couch. Laylee said from the kitchen, "At least get up and take off your work clothes." Something fell on the floor and broke. I called, "Are you ok?" Laylee said, "Oh! My set is ruined!"

"Never mind," I muttered.

I started thinking about Jassem and where I could find him. The last I heard, he said he had bought a few buffalo. We had stayed in touch. We talked once or twice a month. There was only him and Naneh Maryam left, although he had built a cottage beside their old house and moved into it with his bride after their wedding, leaving Naneh Maryam alone in the house. Abdo and I had visited there a few times. Laylee had seen the house too. During the war, we would visit their home when I was on leave. Their mud-brick home was located in a war-torn village located on the outskirts of a date palm grove.

"Get up and have a glass of milk."

Laylee stood above my head holding a tray. I sat up. She was still in her pajamas. I asked, "Is Negar still sleeping?"

She said, "Yes. Whenever she drinks a bottle of milk, it makes her sleep until noon."

She handed me the glass of milk and sat down next to me.

She said, "We've got to find Jassem."

I said, "I have no idea where he is."

She said, "He's probably gone fishing at the Karoon. When we go there next time, we should go with him on a fishing tour. Remember the first time we went, that morning what heavy fog there was by the shore of the Karoon?"

I sipped the glass of milk. I had a bad taste in my mouth, like when you smoke a cigarette before breakfast.

Laylee sat closer to me and continued, "By the way, how did Naneh Maryam's husband die?"

I said, "Jassem said they lined up all the men against a wall and executed them by firing squad. Jassem was just a child then. He and Naneh Maryam fled."

I wasn't in the mood to continue telling the story. I dialed Jassem's house one more time. It rang twice before someone picked up. It was Laiya, Jassem's wife. I said hello and asked how everyone was and then asked, "What's going on? Do you know how Naneh Maryam is doing?"

She burst into tears as soon as she heard this. I asked, "What's wrong, Ms. Laiya? Why are you crying?"

She couldn't muster an answer so I handed the phone to Laylee, but she wasn't able to console Laiya either. I could discern from the half-conversation that Naneh Maryam had been missing for 10 or 12 days until she returned four days ago. That's all.

When Laylee put down the receiver, I asked, "What happened? Did she say much?"

"Didn't you see what state she was in? And carrying a child! Let's call back in a couple of hours."

When Negar started to cry, Laylee got up and went to her. I got up and took out the photo album and sat back down on the couch and started looking at the photographs of the old days.

Naneh Maryam went back to her village to live after they gave the "all clear" and had gained the region back from the hands of the enemy. Abdo insisted that they take Jassem and all go live in a city more distant from the front. Naneh Maryam didn't want to; her heart was with her son, Abdo, and she couldn't bring herself to move away.

We were with Abdo at the war front, until that attack happened in the rolling sand dunes near the border. We were ordered to drive off the enemy and attack them from behind. We attacked at night, but it seemed they were ready for us and had prior intelligence. Bullets were flying everywhere. In the middle of the fight, one or two people saw that Abdo was wounded. He had been shot in his thigh. Our forces retreated but we never saw him again.

Naneh Maryam sank to her knees when they gave her the news. As soon as I could take leave, I went to see Naneh Maryam and Jassem. After you turned off the main road, you had to walk for an hour outside of Karoon to reach their village. In those days there wasn't yet a paved road. I saw Jassem on my way there. He was sitting on the bank while his buffalo grazed in the swamps by the river.

We started walking together through the burnt reed fields and date palm groves together. Naneh Maryam would once in a while sit in front of her home waiting expectantly. She saw us as soon as we emerged from among the reeds, which were as tall as we were. She came running to greet me and hugged me. She had tears in her eyes. She kept asking in a quavering voice, "You haven't seen my Abdo, have you?"

I hadn't seen him. It wasn't like anyone could take care of anyone else in that turmoil. She took me into her home, made a fire and put on the tea but with every move she made, she kept asking about Abdo. "Where on his body was he wounded? Who saw him? Why don't you go and bring my Abdo back? Why did you just leave him in the desert? Did he have food and water?"

Laylee had changed clothes was now sitting next to me. She said, "Haven't you had your milk yet?"

She got up and took the album, closed it, put it on the coffee table and sat back down next to me. We sat silently. Then this time she picked up the album, opened it and thumbed through the pages and asked, "Since when has Naneh Maryam been this way?"

"Since those days."

When we first came back from the front, I used to go to their village often to check on her. Jassem said that Abdo had become Naneh Maryam's every waking thought. He said she would make more food than necessary on the chance that Abdo might show up unannounced. And she would turn down his covers at night so that if he returned late at night, his bed would be ready for him.

I went to see her less often when the war ended. Their village was far away and I could only make it there once or twice a year, and I could only stay two or three days before I had to get back. I also went there for Jassem's wedding. Laylee had wanted to go too, but was pregnant with Negar and wasn't able to make the trip. During those two or three days when I would visit, Naneh Maryam would not say so much as one word. She would only stare blankly into space, and if you didn't call her name, she would stay like that for hours.

I was on the phone until noon, calling and leaving messages for Jassem everywhere and with everyone I knew to call. I also called the office and told them I wouldn't be in, and that I needed to take leave.

The phone rang when I was in the bedroom with Negar. She had started to cry and Laylee was in the kitchen, so I spread out Negar's dolls all over the floor in her room and was entertaining her with them. Laylee answered the phone in the den, and started saying hello as I ran quickly into the den before she called me to the phone. She said, "It's Jassem." And she handed the phone to me. I started to ask how he was when he abruptly started talking about Naneh Maryam. I couldn't believe the things he was telling me, one after the other.

"Naneh went missing ten days ago. We went searching for her everywhere until four days ago, when she returned with a burlap bag full of bones. She had gone near the border on the sand dunes. Both of her feet were badly blistered from walking so far. She said, 'I went after Abdo.' Then she lined up the bones on the bed in the bedroom and covered them with a blanket."

Jassem said, "I don't know what to do. She is ecstatic about Abdo having returned and sleeping in his room, and won't utter a word so as not to wake him. I wanted to collect the bones and take them to be buried somewhere. I don't know whose they are or whether they are Iraqi or Iranian. Naneh won't let me near them. She says, 'Abdo is tired.' She told me, 'After he wakes up, we'll leave this place together.'"

I asked how she was. He said, "Terrible. She won't eat anything. She has locked herself up in that room with Abdo, and only comes out once in a while. When she goes out to the street, she tells the

15

neighbors happily that Abdo has come home. She is in really bad shape. She has gotten much worse since you and Laylee were here and saw her at the New Year."

I said, "Would you like us to come for a visit?"

"What's the use?" he asked. "It would just break your heart. There's no need for that."

I stayed home until sundown, busying myself looking at those albums and playing with Negar. It had just turned nightfall when Jassem called. He was reticent. He just said, "Naneh Maryam has left with the bones." He was worried. He continued, "If you can get yourself over here, please do so."

Laylee packed my bag. I called Jassem's house to let him know I was leaving, when his wife informed me that Jassem and the men from the tribe had followed her footprints into the sea, and that they have all taken lanterns and boats into Karoon to search for Naneh Maryam and Abdo.

Laylee has packed my bag. I will need to leave soon so as not to miss the last train south.

2004

QUAILS

Damn this war that ended so soon. I feel like I've just heard the news that all my loved ones have died. Now what will I do?

I lie down in the bunker and stare at the ceiling. The lines of ceiling joists are there to save us from death. There used to be seven of us in this bunker, but now its just Nasser and me – just the two of us all alone. Our numbers decreased one by one. The guys were either released or wounded or left their corpse behind, like Allah Gholi.

They have ordered us to collect our equipment and retreat. That's the order that makes us want to just die – the order to leave. The truce. Nasser is speechless. All he could say when he first heard was, "Now what do we do?"

I had no answer to give him. What could we do? And what choice did we have?

The whole damn story started that spring day when the walkie-talkie sounded and the commander informed us that one person was being added to our squad. He said to stand outside the bunker and watch for him coming around Death Bend in case he got hit by a mortar shell. It was always the same. Whenever someone was coming, they would order us to keep a lookout for them because Death Bend was in clear sight of the enemy lookout. We used to dread it when they ordered us to retreat for any reason. We would rather have stayed where we were in the bunker than walk around Death Bend where the ground was burned black from being fired upon so many times.

I went out, took refuge amongst the sandbags and waited. Bullets rained down upon Death Bend enveloping it in black gunpowder smoke as he emerged from out of that hateful fog.

He was short, slightly bent over and limped with each step he took. He wore a straw hat instead of a helmet. He walked with his army backpack on his shoulders, totally oblivious to the fact that all this mortar fire was for the purpose of killing him specifically. He didn't even flinch. I called Nasser to come out of the bunker and see this crazy guy.

When he arrived, he said matter-of-factly in his local accent, "Is this my bunker, brother?" It was funny the way he said it. He squinted as he looked down his pimply nose at me. I noticed the sniper rifle on his shoulder. He was the one they had promised to send to us to take out the enemy lookout guard.

Right there, he leaned his gun against the wall of the bunker and brushed the dust off his clothes. We were amazed at how calm he was. We asked his name, to which he responded, "Allah Gholi," and continued to tell us that he had come from one of the villages near Kurd City in central region of the country.

He started working as soon as he set foot inside the bunker without us having said a word or asking him to do anything. He went and found a box that we had emptied of its grenades over the past two or three nights. He tidied up every nook and cranny in the bunker where we had stuffed canned goods and things. Nasser started calling him "Mom" and not only did Allah Gholi not get mad, he started laughing and teasing us back about being helpless, city boys. He put all the stuff into the empty grenade box and made the place look great. Then he sat down and asked, "By the way, what are you two city boys called?"

How quickly we became buddies! He was so down to earth. Nasser and I had long told each other all our stories, and in that desolate place where not a soul could be found, we were excited to hear about his life. Allah Gholi started telling us about being a shepherd in the meadows and the mountains, and helping the animals give birth and milking them. It was around midnight when he got to the subject of

Golchehreh, his fiancé who would always sneak out to meet him in the reed fields.

The next evening at sunset, he asked us to help him write her a letter, as he was illiterate. From that time on, what adventures we had at letter writing! When in the evenings the enemy fire subsided, Allah Gholi would spread out a blanket by the embankment and we would all sit down there. We would put our heads together and start writing the letter. Each one of us would write one part of the letter, and do the best we could to win her heart for Allah Gholi. We would never miss a day writing these letters. Sometimes when we weren't in the mood, Allah Gholi would make us feel guilty by saying, "Well, if you can't, I'll ask the guys in artillery to do it." Then we would give in and sit by the embankment at sunset. What anguish it would be to find new things to say to impress Golchehreh and hear a "Bravo!" from Allah Gholi.

During this time, no response ever came. Allah Gholi said that Golchehreh was also illiterate. Whenever a letter came for her, she would have to come down from the mountain, pick up her mail at the village shop and then find someone literate to read it to her. Once after he returned from leave, he said that Golchehreh had met him at the spring by the foot of the mountain and told him that his letters were lovely but that she was too embarrassed to ask anyone to write down her responses.

Since the time he arrived, he never once took his gun up the embankment. Sometimes Nasser and I would ask him why he was sent to us. He was fascinated by the plains that were green when he arrived but dried out with the summer heat. He loved the quails that lived among the dry grass a little further off. When we were in the bunker in the hot afternoons, they would sneak over and steal a nice drink of water from the tank.

That water tank was right in front of our bunker. We had covered it with sandbags lest a piece of shrapnel puncture a hole in it. Each day the water tanker truck would come by and fill it up. Allah Gholi dug an irrigation canal to channel to reclaim the used, daily water. When he returned from leave, he planted cucumbers, tomatoes and squash along the sides of that canal.

Later on, we realized that while we were napping at noon, he would open the tank faucet on purpose and let it drip. At noon, he would peek out of the bunker to watch for the quails. One day when I couldn't fall asleep, I went and sat down next to him to see what he was watching. I saw the quails bustling in the shade under the wide, squash plant leaves. Allah Gholi whispered that he had planted the squash plants especially for them. He mimicked the call of the quails with his mouth and went out of the bunker and sat down next to the water tank. From where he was sitting, he looked at me smugly for not understanding and appreciating the things he loved.

Then the commanders issued an all-alert and ordered a raid on the enemy embankment. It was that night when we attacked. He was still wearing his straw hat. He rationalized, "Who knows where we'll be tomorrow and besides, the sun is blistering hot."

When we emerged from out of our embankment there were tens of hundreds of rifles and heavy machine guns firing at us in the flat, thorny plains. We all got down to the ground and when the number of our casualties got too high, the commander ordered a retreat. Those of us who survived, returned.

When we got back to the bunker, we waited. None of them were back yet. Nasser got back first. He was bloody and exhausted. He had carried a wounded soldier on his back all the way back.

Allah Gholi never came back. When it got light outside, we went up the embankment and saw him through our binoculars sprawled out on the ground at the enemy embankment. The straw hat was still on his head. We could see the brim flapping in the morning breeze.

Nasser and I were both numb with disbelief until that evening. At sunset, we remembered Golchehreh who was surely anticipating a letter from him. At first we weren't sure what to do, but then Nasser went and brought back a pen and piece of paper. I spread out the blanket by the embankment. We got busy writing the letter.

Now that the war is over, there is no longer any impediment to retrieving his body. In the morning, the walkie-talkie rang again. It was our commander who said that he had had a discussion with the enemy commander and the plan was for us to go and retrieve the bodies of our soldiers. We took our white flags and left.

His corpse was still there. We knew right where to find it. Every day at sunset after the postman picked up our letters, we would go up the embankment and without saying a word, we would check on him through our binoculars.

Allah Gholi's face had decomposed. We walked through bevies of quails surrounding him. We covered his face with a handkerchief and put his body onto a stretcher and carried him back. His body is still there on the stretcher outside the bunker.

The two of us are still dumbfounded. The war is over, otherwise, his body would still by lying by that embankment and Nasser and I would still be writing letters to Golchehreh every day.

What a beautiful sunset this is. Damn the war that ended so soon.

2003

A DOG'S LIFE

For a moment I pause in front of the huge entrance door and take a deep breath before going inside, but I don't give myself the chance to hesitate any longer or wonder whether I should go in or not, or even ask myself if it is worth all the trouble or not. If I pause, I might get cold feet or even abandon the whole idea but then everything I had set my hopes upon would go up in smoke.

I step inside. There is a long corridor with a hubbub of people coming and going like columns of ants. Many are missing limbs. Some look down the endless hallway with an errant eye, and I can tell right away by the fixed pupil that their eye is artificial.

Wearing red uniforms with faded, fringed epaulets, the guards stand on either side of the doorway to keep out strangers. One of them comes forward and asks me where I'm going and who I'm there to see. I say nothing as I hand him my application. He reads it and says, "Wing 12, Room 322."

I start walking down the main corridor that feels like a big tunnel. I look down this long, main hallway with its yellow walls but don't see an end to it through the crowds of people with disabilities; I just see the many wings and hundreds of rooms. The ceiling is high with yellow lamps hanging down and tens or hundreds of ceiling fans spinning and swaying from side to side. Gathered outside the closed doors of the rooms, people shout to hear one another.

I find wing 12. There are rooms on either side of the hallway with people waiting outside the doors. Some of the people are missing a leg, or are blinded in one eye, and some are blind in both eyes, indicated by the white cane in their hands. They all talk loudly as if they are in some kind of a contest against each other. Some argue with the person sitting next to them and some talk to or even argue with themselves.

The number 322 is written above the door of the eleventh room, where a crowd is gathered outside. I grip my application form tightly so as not to lose it in the commotion. I stand in the crowd and wait in limbo. Some speak softly. A man whose leg was amputated at the knee pounds on the door and shouts. I look at him and listen to what he and the others are saying when they suddenly open the door and the crowd pushes its way into the room. The room is filled with men with disabilities.

We surround a man sitting at an old, makeshift wooden desk in the middle of a bare room. We hold out our application forms all talking to him at once about our cases. He gets up and yells at us, "Hand me your applications! How many hands do you think I have here?! They regulate new benefits every day without even consulting with us!"

He chatters on while we quietly stand against the dirty, yellow walls of that bare, chair-less room, waiting for our turns while one person goes around collecting the applications. The man gradually becomes engrossed in the application forms and we begin whispering. One tells how he found out about it, and another says how happy he is that they called him in early – for they're sure to cancel the benefits program in a few days.

People begin to talk and their chatter fills the room. The noise brings on a panic attack and I see the dismembered people again. That voice inside my head tells me to attack them. I hold my hands at my sides tightly, for the doctor has told me not to listen to that voice. I try instead to think of something else. I try to think about Nader. Everything started when he arrived. He is how I got to this point.

The air was warm. Yes, the air was very warm and I got so hot in this room that my ears started ringing and the room started spinning. I wanted to quickly get my mind on something else, but couldn't as I called out to my wife Maryam, and when she came to me I saw her in pieces. I went towards her but don't remember anything after that. When I came to, I realized the poor woman had picked me up and laid me against the pile of bedding in the corner of the room. She was in the middle of the room scrubbing the carpet. I must have vomited all over the room.

When I moved, she turned to look at me and I saw her bloody lip and the welts of my handprint on her cheek. She told me someone was waiting at the door for me even though she had told them I was not well.

I got up, went to the door and saw Nader standing there. I couldn't believe that he would come there to see me at that time of night in his feeble condition walking on two canes. I asked him inside but he refused, and I didn't insist. We just sat down on the ground outside the front door and started reminiscing about the past and our war memories about our old buddies from back then. Some of them we both knew, some of them only I knew and some others only Nader knew. A few stray dogs grew near to us as we talked. When they came too close we threw pebbles in their direction. Nader grew sentimental thinking about the old days when he still had two legs and so many friends. Then he told me he had come to give me some important news that having a grave in the city cemetery had been recently added to the benefits we received and so on and so forth, and the difference between the benefits we get and the going market rates. He said we could easily sell right then for double the price and maybe even more. I stood there in the dark after he left listening to the dogs and thinking about Maryam...

There was uproar inside the room as one of the men who appeared to be in better condition than any of us suddenly fell to the floor and started convulsing and foaming at the mouth. The man, still sitting at his desk, picked up a red telephone receiver and called for help.

We all surround the man. One person starts rubbing his shoulders and another rubs his legs and another person goes to fetch a glass of water for him. He throws up, spraying white and pink liquid all over the room as a sour stench fills the air. Before he regains consciousness and the person who went to fetch the water returns, two people who were called for help show up, pick him up by two arms and legs and drag him out like a slaughtered lamb.

The man at the desk calls us up one by one as soon as he is finished with the documents, and hands them to each of us. The document of the man who had the seizure is left there on the desk, when one of the others grabs it and starts running toward wing 13, room 154.

The hallways are still crowded, people are still standing outside the doors pounding on them and shouting to be heard.

We line up outside room 154 and go inside one by one to get our documents signed. The man who had a seizure returns. He looks pale and chalky and still has vomit on his collar. We don't let him stand at the end of the line but let him go first so that he can be done all the sooner. He is listless as he leans against the wall and stares up at the ceiling fans, and I don't know who, but somebody asked, "How much will they pay for it?"

Suddenly everybody answers in unison as if they had rehearsed it a hundred times, "Double the price! You could even sell the document!"

And then in the middle of all that chatter and tumult in the crowded hallway, one of them announces like a choir soloist, "It says in the circular that you can select the location of your grave. People buy the ones near the road more easily, no matter whether they are one or two level graves. It's better to find the buyer first, then when you do the transaction, you can immediately register it in the buyer's name."

The choir soloist is still talking as my turn comes up. I go inside and hand them my document. They sign the bottom, stamp it and hand it back to me. I tuck the document deep down into my pocket as I walk out of the office so that I won't lose it if I have a seizure.

The man who had a seizure passes me as I walk briskly down the dark, yellow corridor. I pick up my pace so as not to be left behind.

2003

STAMPS

Nobody knows what happened to Idris – not even his aging mother who comes out to the alley at sunset, takes him by the hand and leads him back home. It's nothing anyone would be proud of knowing for me to be proud of knowing it. Idris has become a slovenly, spacey creature that ventures out in the evenings to the park north of our neighborhood. He sits over in that corner of the park with the best view to watch the sun go down. The people in our neighborhood know exactly what happens next. From the moment the sun begins to disappear over the horizon and inches out of sight, Idris takes on a strange quality. His face grows redder and redder until for a moment he looks like a blister about to burst. He yells and thrashes about and utters words that no one has ever been able to understand. Then his elderly mother approaches Idris. Weeping, she takes his hand and leads him home.

That's why I never stick around in the evenings. I get the heck out of our tight, narrow alleyway. I feel like packing up all my things and running away to any place but here. I will take everything except these stamp collections with me. These are the last ties connecting me to that half-opened, second story window across the alley - a window that nobody has opened or closed for years. And no matter how I have tried, all I have seen in it were the memories of my childhood. And now that the coals are burning in this broiler, I'm facing that same window now, about to separate myself from it all forever.

This old window encompasses all of my very first memories of childhood. From the earliest days I can remember, Idris was my buddy, as all of us kids grew up together in this tight alleyway. Our houses faced one another and from as far back as I can remember, you could easily see into his window from our courtyard. And I can remember Idris and Roya hanging out of the window picking persimmons off the branches that spilled into the alleyway, and this is why I love the autumn. The persimmons ripen and blush, like a young girl staring into the eyes of a boy peeking out from behind the fruit laden branches to get a good look at her.

My childhood began with Idris, Roya and the other children in our alleyway and ended like the stamps that will go up in smoke in the blink of an eye as I slowly place them into the fire. As we grew older we found that gradually we were standing in lines that separated the girls from the boys. It was in vengeance of that segregation that I lay in wait for Roya to peek out of the window. I aimed at her from the branches of the persimmon tree and threw a rock at her. The rock hit her brow and I caught a glimpse of her face and clothes covered in blood. It left behind a reminder of the old days; a scar, which I saw for the last time by the stop sign.

Every morning she would tie her hair back with a yellow ribbon before going to school. She was always home by noon. In the afternoons, as a way to get back at me for throwing the stone at her, she would peek out the window and look down the alleyway, ignoring me on purpose to make me jealous. On some excuse, I would come down and open the courtyard door to find nobody out in the alley. Then I would hear Roya laughing hysterically and look up to find that she was no longer in the window, but rather inside her room, laughing even more loudly to make me even more angry.

Burn stamp, burn! This was a stamp Idris had bought in October after the revolution. He said, "Now that there's a revolution going on, you can find these stamps everywhere!"

Burn stamp, burn! And this stamp is the first one they published after the revolution. Idris had told me about it a just few days before when he said, "We have to get these for sure and get a lot of them because they will be worth a lot someday! Look at the stamps of the French Revolution or the Russian Revolution! Whoever has those stamps now is in the money!"

Burn stamp, burn! Burn! Burn!

We all got older and everyone went their separate ways. I would see Roya going around in her white tennis shoes and her short grey coat passing out different flyers. But Idris and I kept our album together and never once thought about dismantling and separating it. Roya was the link between Idris and me, even though she and I still weren't talking because of the grudge she held against me for the rock-throwing incident, but every once in awhile, our eyes spoke a few words with one another. Idris and I were putting new stamps into the album one day, when Roya came in to help us for the first time, and without saying a word, she handed me one of the flyers to read.

I didn't read it. I looked at her face and saw the scar on her left brow and wished that I could turn back time to when we were children, just as I have wished a thousand times since that day at the stop sign. I wish I had never thrown that stone. I wish there had never been the window.

Roya gave us an Italian stamp, an image of a girl and a boy with their heads on each other's shoulders and cupid's arrow through both of their hearts and a drop of blood dripping from the tip of the arrow.

We kept the albums at their house and I don't know why, but I wanted to get that album from Idris. This upset him, and he told me to go ahead and take them both, which I didn't do. Later on whenever I turned the pages of that album I would see that Italian stamp turned over. I would quickly flip past that page and neither of us would say a word. But every so often when I was heartsick and Idris wasn't in the room, I would turn back to that page and steal a glance. That's why I took it out of the third album, to burn it last of all.

The next day Roya went missing. Nobody saw her or found any sign of her. These people had changed; they weren't like the people of two or three years prior. Idris would go straight home each day with a newspaper in hand. He wouldn't say anything and I wouldn't ask, but I knew well what he was looking for. I was also getting a newspaper everyday and looking amongst the names of the homicides, executions or people killed in street violence looking for her name. But there was never any sign of her.

After that, Idris grew distant from all the other kids on the block and stayed inside, but I remained his friend. I used the stamp collection as the excuse to keep seeing him. I would turn the city upside down in search of new stamps to buy and take to Idris and put them into the album and talk to him and get some kind of response out of him. I bought this Greek stamp right around that time even though

I knew it was highway robbery. I bought it anyway for its novelty and perhaps it would make my childhood friend happy for just a moment. And now I'm putting it into the fire so that this Greek goddess of love and hate will burn and die.

After the war started, I pulled every string and finally succeeded in being sent to the front. The enemy had invaded our country in Khorramshahr, which meant "green city", but it came to be known as "bloody city". This shook me to the bone.

I saw Idris much less after that, only when I was on leave, or in the streets or alleyway, or whenever he peeked out of the second floor window across from me. My mother would report to me that neither mother nor son ever left the house. Especially since their house was tagged with a red x and graffiti which no one could read. Mother said that mother and son had spent one night until morning scrubbing it off the wall outside their house. The color went away but the vague impression will always be there.

It was the last year of the war. I was on leave. One morning someone knocked at the front door. My mother opened it and was surprised as she told me Idris wanted to see me. This surprised me too as we hadn't seen each other in a year. I went to the door. He was holding our stamp collection in his arms. We sat down on the carpet in the living room. He said he brought the albums for me to divvy up. I knew this wasn't about the stamp collection, because he knew how several years of war had aged me and he must have known that I was not interested in stamp collecting anymore. He finally admitted that he wanted to come to the front. He had gone to the recruitment office and they performed a background check on him in our neighborhood, but he did not pass muster. I think it was the month of June. I was dying to turn the pages of the stamp album to the Italian stamp with the girl and the boy whose hearts were pinned together.

I couldn't wait. I turned the pages and got to the stamp, which wasn't face down. I could tell by the marking left from its position on the page all those years that the stamp recently had been turned over. My hands were shaking and I could see Idris watching me out of the corner of his eye. Then he turned his head. I stared at the stamp and raised my head up and looked at the window across the alley. Idris showed me the other stamps. He said that he had not done any more collecting and the albums were still incomplete. He went on and on. I was burning up. I wanted so much to ask about Roya but my tongue and lips wouldn't move.

The next day we went to the recruitment center. I provided him a reference, which they confirmed, due to my service of several years at the war front. When my leave was over, we went together back to the war front. From then on, we went back to being the same old friends we had always been to each other, even though Idris was still quiet and reserved.

It was then when we bought this stamp, in Kermanshah. Perhaps we wanted to relive the old times when we went to the post office at Azadi Square. Idris first bought a set, and then went back again and bought a second set, saying that he had forgotten how we had always bought the stamps in our collection in sets of two. Now this fire will consume these stamps and separate me from that time of my life forever. I will keep on burning these stamps until I forget all of these memories. As I sit by this fire today, I will recall all the old memories one last time so that I can forget them once and for all.

They said the peace resolution agreement had been signed. It was exactly forty days after we returned to the front when they announced this. We were preparing to go home. The war was ending and I had no reason to stay in that strange province. Idris was returning with me, since I was the only reason he went there to begin with. We were at the Koozeran camp between Islamabad and Kermanshah. We headed for home after we got our documents signed.

We walked down a dirt road that led to the highway, which was a couple of miles away. We walked peacefully through an old, oak forest. There was no need to hurry. There was no particular job waiting for us back in our city. Neither of us knew what we wanted to do after the war was over. We talked about our childhood, about the present and about what the future would bring. Idris suggested that we sell our stamp collection and use the capital for investments, and we laughed at the preposterousness of our pipe dreams.

We could hear the sound of shooting getting louder. It was coming from afar off, near the highway. I presumed that the forces that were being released were probably emptying their ammunition on the way home, and Idris teased that these would be the war stories that they would tell their grandchildren to prove their bravery and courage.

The sound of the shooting got louder and clearer as we got closer to the highway. It seemed like war again. I said to Idris, "There's no reason for war after peace." And he remarked, "You who were our fiercest fighter, had your bags packed to go home the moment the war ended! It's not like we have anybody more combative than you!" We laughed and rested for a while under an old oak tree, heedless to the sound of the gunfire near the road, which we thought had nothing to do with us. We started walking to get to the main road before dark, and from there we would go to Kermanshah, and then to our own town.

We could see the highway as we came around the last bend of the mountain road. Everything was chaos. Some were going, some were coming, there were soldiers by the road walking hunched over, and some were lying down loading their guns. We walked faster to get there quick and see what was going on. A few people yelled at us to get down or we'd get shot, and didn't we see that it was war?

We were dazed and confused. Was this any time for war? From that moment on, Idris was quiet. We started walking ahead when they told us to be careful, that those people also speak Farsi. We didn't stop, but continued on. I wish we hadn't. If we had not gone forward, everything would be completely different now, and maybe even Idris and I would be selling these stamps and starting a business, and he would not be like this, and I wouldn't be in such anguish.

And now I will burn these stamps that we bought during those happy and blissful times when we were weaving dreams, oblivious to everything as we sat there talking in that oak forest. I will burn them to remove my connection to those sweet times. And the fire in this broiler consuming these stamps flares and flames and burns all of those dreams to ash.

The way back was closed. We hunkered down in the battlefield. We slept under a bridge that night near the corpse of one of the enemy women soldiers. We could tell by the long chestnut hair that it was a woman, otherwise, her face was destroyed. People there said that a grenade had exploded in her face and it was completely gone. Her cotton flower-colored skull was visible. Idris looked at it and grew nauseated. I took him away from there and he heaved as his face turned white as chalk. I said, "Let's get back to the camp and stay there until the war ends and the roads open." But he didn't want to. He wanted to stay there and go a little further in the morning towards home, to start our work and our life. When he said this, he had a bitter smile on his face. He looked me in the eyes and when I saw how

40

sick he was, I decided we would stay there together under that bridge near the other soldiers who had gathered there.

This morning, mother started talking about how I should get married now that I have served several years at the war front, and have been given a managerial position at the bank and so on. And I know she won't let up this time and will keep noodling me until she gets a positive answer.

But I'm still staring at the window across the alley, warming myself with the heat radiating from the fire in the broiler, looking up at the ripe persimmons, which mother still won't pick for fear of me. The birds start in on them and she then gets upset and nags me about being no less important to me than Idris, and why shouldn't a person pick God's fruit? And that God doesn't like waste and a thousand other reasons and excuses.

In the morning they said that they were retreating and the forces had been deployed by helicopter and positioned behind them. The sound of the shooting grew distant. I don't know why Idris wanted to pull me into the battle at the war front.

We started out toward the front and saw the locals here and there all over the place. Some were examining the corpses of the soldiers to see what valuables could be taken. There were corpses of men and women everywhere on the side of the road. You could tell which ones were women by their long hair. But all of their faces were destroyed.

The sound of shooting grew louder and louder. There were forces along the road on the ground and the commanders were ordering them around the hill to ambush and kill every last one of those unsuspecting people. We were shot at by heavy machine gun fire. We went down the trench by the road sign until the gunfire let up.

I don't know why I feel cold. I just want to throw all of these stamps into the fire to warm me, but I don't throw them in. This ruthless pain and anguish must leave me piece by piece. I am not strong enough to recall all these memories and put them out of my mind all at once. I can't, I'm not able to, I'm helpless and alone; I'm so alone. All I have are a world full of memories that I'm trying to escape from.

Over there by us at the foot of a road sign was the body of a woman splayed out on the ground. Her hands were outstretched, she was wearing no dress and her disheveled hair was covering her face. Her body and neck were full of red splotches and bruises and her lips were purple.

The shooting grew heavier and everyone got onto the ground. I crawled up next to that woman's corpse as the shooting grew even louder. The soldiers by the roadside attacked, yelled, shot their weapons and fought hand-to-hand combat. Then came the sounds of moaning and groaning. I didn't raise my head to see what was going on. I just stayed there until the shooting quieted down and the battle moved to the other side of the hill.

When I dared raise my head, I immediately saw Idris, his face pale, trembling like a willow tree, his lips quivering, and I realized he was panicking but I didn't know why. I thought it was from looking at the corpse that was shielding me. I said, "Let's move on" but Idris was frozen in his place. I repeated, "Let's go!" and took his hand to lead him away, but he wouldn't move. He grabbed my wrist and just said, "Roya."

This word shocked me. I began to shake when I heard that name, especially in the battlefield, in the middle of all that chaos. I didn't understand what he was trying to say and I didn't understand that he was talking about the body. I said, "Roya, what?" Then he didn't say anything. He just stared at the body. I turned toward the corpse when Idris took my face in his two hands and pleaded with me not to look. I froze as my legs gave way under me. And I realized that the person that had been shielding me from the bullets was Roya.

Now I understood Idris. I became just like him. I was right next to the girl from my childhood who would hang out of the second story window to pick persimmons and laugh. I would climb up the tree and bend the branches toward her so she could reach them and pick the fruit. The same fruit that I wouldn't let anyone pick after I returned. The same fruit that only the birds were allowed to eat. The fruit would remain on the branches until the cold and snow and blizzards would bring the ice.

I wanted to turn around again but Idris said, "This is my sister" but how could I not turn around and not look at her? I told Idris to spare me. I was in such bad shape that he felt sorry for me and released me, taking his hands off of my face. I slowly turned around like I was about to behold the most delicate creature on earth; a creature that would break if I even bat an eyelash. I looked at her. Yes, it was Roya. I reached out my trembling hand and moved the tangled hair out of her face. I saw the scar above her left eyebrow, seeing myself and seeing her and seeing the rock that was thrown from the courtyard, and seeing her lifeless body. I saw everything in that moment. My back broke and I broke and I died in that moment. Roya had aged, just as I had. She was looking away and averting her glance from me as if shy, toward the hills and the crooked oaks.

I don't know how long we lingered beside her. A few of the local youth appeared, gawking and sneering at the dead body. Idris and I were the only ones mourning her death. We were in such shock, filled with grief and sadness that we never even thought to cover her up so that the sun would not burn her and bother her. In those moments, I saw my whole life pass before my eyes, a second time, a third time, a hundredth time, and a thousandth time. I saw my own past and I wished I could have cried and lessened the burden of grief, but the well of tears had dried up from holding them back for so long.

The war moved forward, the roads opened and grew busy and it was no place to remain any longer. Idris took off his shirt and covered her body. He picked up her legs and pulled her into the ditch across from there. I didn't offer to help him. I saw a few more local youths talking and motioning at Idris. I stayed there by the road sign and watched Idris who pulled Roya into the trench until I could no longer see him. I don't know what happened after that. Like now that I am grieving and all life has lost its meaning. I couldn't stay there any longer. I got up from where I was sitting by that road sign. I went limping up that hill to see Idris and Roya one more time and drown in my childhood memories and cry, if the tears would come.

Idris was kneeling on the dirt, clawing away at the ground with his bare hands. Roya was laid out next to him, with her arms outstretched, as if all of the bullets that were shot at us were wedding rice and she was dancing.

Idris' shirt had fallen away from her body and it burned me when I saw and imagined how she died, and after her death, what she experienced in preparation for burial. Idris kept clawing and I could see his digging had turned the ground to a mixture of dirt and blood. The grave of my childhood dream – Roya's grave - had turned crimson with his blood. Idris dug that humble grave all day long until sunset. Then he picked up his sister's body and placed her inside it. He straightened her hair and covered her face, and then covered her over with dirt. All that remained was a dirt mound, the only sign left of a girl named Roya who was no more.

I went down to Roya's grave. Idris was kneeling with his forehead on the mound, but he wasn't crying. His face showed no emotion except that he was as white as chalk. I took his hand to raise him up, but he wouldn't move. His fingertips were torn up. There was whitish flesh, skin and bone hanging like claws sunken into and pulled out from a carcass, dripping flesh and skin and blood. He had no fingertips or nails or bone; the skin and flesh hanging there was a mixture of dirt and sand and blood. I raised him up. This tragedy was more momentous than something causing merely sorrow or disgust.

It was now dark. We came slowly up out of the ditch, flagged down the first car that would pick up passengers. We went to Kermanshah, got on a bus and headed for home. When we got to our town, I escorted Idris to our alley and without a word, we separated and each went home.

From that day on, Idris has been the same. I have aged a lot, quite a lot, more than people my age by what I've been through. And now that I've collected everything under this persimmon tree in the courtyard, and have thrown all the stamps into the broiler, except this one, I'm going to finally forget everything by telling the story to someone to get it off my chest once and for all. I'll throw the last stamp into the fire, get up and leave before mother returns and nags me, asking me why I didn't show up at work on the first day.

I must go. I hope the road sign is still there.

1999

THE TICKET

As I walked out of the bank, I noticed that it had started to snow. I looked at my watch. I was lucky to have been able to get a taxi early that morning and be first in line at the bank. I was able to get the check cashed quickly. Now I'm sure I'll have the money in the account by the time the checks clear.

Snowflakes are falling on the ground. The snow beats down heavily for a while and then it stops. That two or three month's time was a good experience. Now I am able to tell the difference between rainclouds and regular clouds.

I'm sure I won't be sorry I didn't bring an umbrella. If I had lugged one along for just a few snowflakes, I wouldn't have been able to carry this big envelope of money. That unconscionable teller at the bank told me they hadn't received delivery of any new bills and so he stuffed a large envelope full of old small, worn out bills and handed it to me. I run out to the street and look again at my watch. No need to worry about the time. "Sir, Sir, Mr. Faramarz!" I turn around and look at him carefully for a moment, "Hey Biabani! Is that you?"

He stands there in disbelief on the other side of the slimy gutter staring gaping-mouthed at me. He is wearing a long, khaki-colored trench coat. His beard has turned salt and pepper and his eyes are puffy underneath. He looks at me with that stupid look on his face.

I stand there waiting for him to come over to my side of the gutter. He plods across like someone carrying a lot of extra weight. He hangs his arms around me in an embrace and hugs me and kisses my cheek.

"How've you been, Biabani? I haven't forgotten your name! Ramezan Biabani, right?"

He holds my face in his two palms nodding his head. I pull back to get free. I pat him firmly on his shoulder with my free hand. I say, "Where have you been? What are you doing here?"

I don't wait for his answer. I turn my head to keep an eye out for a passing jitney. "I'm sure you haven't had any more broken fingers since then, right?"

I look down at his finger. It had healed crookedly. He smiled wistfully.

I had known Ramezan Biabani during the war. He was a simple office worker that seemed a little slow. It would be an understatement to say he loved the warfront, war, shooting and guns. What he really loved most were the guys there. He was deployed to the front despite having a wife and four small children – of course that was the headcount at the time. He would stay seven or eight months on each deployment instead of three months, which was the expected duration of any volunteer deployment. He wasn't a member of any battery or detachment. When the forces went up to the front line, he would stay back and keep watch over the tents and equipment. He never failed to cry incessantly for days each time we'd return. A few of the soldiers were always martyred each time and when he would hear the news of this, he'd cry like a baby and wipe his nose with his sleeve.

"Taxi! Taxi! I'm going straight!"

The jitney stopped up ahead. I hide the large envelope under my arm to keep it dry. I hesitate, "Well, it was nice seeing you Biabani. I've got to go but you can ride along with me if you want?"

He drops his head and starts following me without saying a word. Three passengers are already sitting in the back of the jitney, so we squeeze into the front. I sit next to the driver with my package on my knees, while Biabani sits next to the window. The driver isn't easily able to change gears, so I scoot over closer to Biabani. I ask him, "So where do you live? Where are you working now?"

It's so tight that I can see him only through the driver's rear view mirror.

"Nowhere – they've suspended me from my job. I'm unemployed," he answers, conspicuously lowering his voice.

We're stuck in traffic. I look at my watch. I still have plenty of time.

I ask, "Why? What for?"

He replies, "I'm surprised you haven't heard. Everybody seems to know these days that the miserable fellow, Biabani has lost everything."

I was surprised by his tone. I ask, "What do you mean? What happened?"

It was like he was waiting for me to ask this very question, for him to pour out his heart to me.

"You know, Faramarz, I have put in 29 years at my job. Exactly 29 years, three months and six days to now. But up to the time I was still employed, it was exactly 28 years, one month and 27 days."

The traffic is moving slowly. I look at the huge snowflakes. They are pushing for a grand finale. It reminds me of when our battalion was attacking in the west of the country. That's when I really became an expert on the weather. What a heavy snow it was! The mules would freeze to death on their feet.

"One day my sister came to our office. She said she knew someone from whom she could purchase televisions at below market price. She talked to everyone in the office; they were mostly women. Just a few others and myself were the only men in the office. She talked to them and collected money from them. Of course they wouldn't have given her any money if it had not been for the fact that she was my sister. The televisions were delivered in one month. It was wonderful. The TV's were twenty to thirty thousand tomans under market price. This was a big difference with the going rate in the bazaar."

The traffic came to a stop again. I was supposed to catch a city bus when I reached the square. I'm glad that I had found this one ticket at the bottom of my pocket; otherwise I would have had to waste a lot of time going to the other side of the square to buy a bus ticket.

"My sister came back once more to the office. This time, she didn't even stop by my office - me, her brother - to see me! My co-workers all trusted her with their money right there at the door. I found out about it only when people who missed out last time were handing me money to give to her. Well, I was their colleague. I was too embarrassed to admit to them that I hadn't been to her house even once since the New Year. I went over to her house to deliver the money to her. She smiled and hugged me and thanked me. There were exactly 73 people. After some time, my co-workers started coming by my office to ask me what news I had about the televisions from my sister. I told them I only knew what they knew. One day when they started complaining, I went over to my sister's house again to get some news. Her husband was there with the children. When I asked to see her, he said indignantly and abruptly that she had left him two weeks ago and that he had no news of her. At first I was in shock but then I started to cry. It dawned on me that she had run off with the money."

A layer of snow had stuck to the sidewalk. With this one snowfall, people would surely be caught off guard and arrive at the bank later. I hope it snows even more.

"They issued a complaint against me, and I was arrested for aiding and abetting a fraudster. I went to jail for three months. Think about it. I stayed in jail the same amount of time as one deployment to the war front! Everybody knew I was innocent, but they said they were holding me there in order to compel my sister to turn herself in."

I looked at myself in the rear view mirror. I saw him crying, just like the times when he would hear the news of the guys having been martyred. We even played a trick on him once. The commander of our battalion was a man by the name of Javad Bozorgzadegan. Biabani loved him a lot. Bozorgzadegan had gone on an enemy reconnaissance mission to the front line. We all gathered in tents and sat with our heads lowered somberly. Abbas Kian went and brought Biabani into the tent. A couple of people were fake crying. I was watching him out of the corner of my eye. He was in shock. He fell to his knees in front of the very first person sitting by the door and stared at him. The man covered his face with both of his hands and said that Javad Bozorgzadegan had stepped on a mine and was blown to pieces. Biabani cried for two days and didn't eat one bite of food. We didn't say a word, but carried on the charade until the day Bozorgzadegan returned.

"They put up bail and I got out. Then they suspended me from my job. It has now been one year and one month since I lost my job. I have asked everyone I know for money. And do you know where I have just been? I just came back from seeing Abbas Kian. "

They brought the news that Biabani would be returning to the front. That news spread quickly. Whenever he would come, we would tease him ruthlessly for laughs. As soon as he arrived at the camp, he would kiss and hug and ask each one of us how we were. He hadn't even gotten to our tent yet when I saw two people were carrying him under his arms over to the clinic. Face lit up, Abbas Kian came running to tell us the juicy story that "as soon as Biabani got here, he held out his hand to shake hands and put his arms around my shoulders and get my face all slobbery, and I took his big finger and twisted it so hard that it popped!"

"I've been unemployed for one year and with eight tiny mouths to feed! I've gone to see everyone I know. I've sold all of my belongings. Do you remember when we went to the west? It was the first time Bozorgzadegan had invited me to participate in the operation. He gave me a mule and designated me as its commander. I was supposed to bring food and passengers back and forth on it. On the night of the attack, I had packed everything onto the mule. Do you remember? It was at the Olaghoo peak where Abbas Kian got hit in the head by shrapnel.

"We were moaning as we went forward. One of the enemy soldiers positioned in a ditch on the side of the road and threw a grenade at us. I got down on the ground but I heard Abbas yell just once – just one scream. I went to him. He was unconscious. I thought he was going to die but I bandaged his head anyway. The forces went forward but I stayed behind in that commotion. I saw Ramezan Biabani. The mule wasn't moving forward. Biabani was pulling on the reins and yelling at it saying that if it didn't move forward, he'd issue a complaint to the commander and if the mule only knew what a bad-tempered man that commander was!

"I called out to him. We helped each other get Abbas Kian onto the mule's back. I thought if we could get him back to camp sooner, he might live. On the way, the mule was hit by shrapnel and fell to the ground. No matter what we did, it wouldn't get up. I began to cry and pleaded with the mule, 'Just get Kian to the camp clinic. It's for your own good too. They'll take care of your wound there.' But the mule wouldn't get up. I took Kian on my back and started walking. I didn't know where I was going. I just kept walking to and fro, to and fro, from the beginning of the night until dawn. I was afraid to stop and rest for fear this young man would die on my watch. We finally reached the clinic. The doctor seeing Abbas

Kian said if we had gotten there a half an hour later...."

The traffic has died down. I don't know why I did something so stupid as to write today's date on the checks. I could have at least given myself time to pay for these ten back tires until next week.

"I went to Kian. I told him what happened. I was embarrassed to ask for money, but I did. I had no choice. We were completely out of rice, oil and meat. I asked him to loan me 100,000 tomans but he thought I was joking. Then he said his financial situation was not good in this recession, and finally he put 2000 tomans into my fist and told me I didn't have to pay him back. But I handed it right back to him and left. But at his door I said..."

He was crying again. I elbowed him in the side with the arm that was holding the envelope of money and whispered to him to control himself and quiet He whispered back to me, "Was his life worth less than 100,000, 50,000 or even 20,000 tomans? What if that night I had...?"

We were pulling into the square. I struggled to reach into my pocket to pay the driver. I said, "We'll get out here." Biabani also got out.

While I was paying the rest of the money to the driver, he whispered in my ear, "If you have any way to help me, I mean, just a loan, God willing, when I go back to work..."

I look across the road. The bus is full. I've got to board this bus. I won't get there in time if I wait around for the next bus. "Yes, for sure! You have a phone, right? Give me your number and I'll call you. I will surely find a way to help you. Do you have any paper? I'll call you. I'll call you tomorrow or at the very latest, the day after tomorrow."

I was trying to find something to write on and he was fumbling around in his pockets to find a piece of paper. I say, "Here, let me write it on the back of this ticket. What is your number?" The city bus is revving the engines. I write down his phone number hurriedly. I'm trying to leave but he is hanging on my neck.

"Please do whatever you can for me."

I say, "Don't worry about a thing. It is my duty to help you." I release myself from his grip and say goodbye.

I jump onto the bus right as the bus doors close.

1998

THE MERMAID

All three of us had been hit by shrapnel. We were taken to the field hospital behind the front. The shrapnel had wounded me in the abdomen and they were forced to remove three feet of my intestines. Mirza had to have both of his legs amputated below the knees. Davood had taken shrapnel to the eyes. The doctors held out hope that he would improve. But for now, both of his eyes were bandaged up.

The three of us were lying on our beds and could not leave the room. The only activity we had to keep us busy was watching the nurses through the half-open door of our room pushing beds with the wounded to and fro. They transferring the wounded immediately from the front line battles into this field hospital behind the front line, so these people were still in their army uniforms. There were first aid bandages on their faces and tourniquets on their arms. The field hospital was a holy mess. They had even put beds along the hallways that quickly became occupied with people who were torn apart by bullets and metal shrapnel. The three of occupied a room with dingy grey walls splattered with blood that made you sick to look at as we drowned ourselves in memories of times before we were injured. It was as if room 324 was the beginning and end of the world.

At first, none of us paid any attention to the girlish voice on the loudspeaker calling the doctors to emergency surgery or alerting them to patients being discharged from the hospital. But little by little, that voice grew on all three of us. We never said anything about it to each other, but whenever her voice came over the loudspeaker as she made the announcements, our hearts would pound as we all stopped talking so that we could hear her, and it was obvious how each of us felt. We gradually started getting to know each other and talking about what our lives were like before we got injured. We quit watching the newly wounded being admitted to the hospital. Any chance we would get, we would try to pull the discussion back to her.

Each one of us had created a vision of her in our minds. I imagined her having a small, innocent-looking face with big brown eyes, perhaps younger than us, although we were not more than seventeen or eighteen years old at the time. Mirza would describe her with a mole on her cheek below her mouth. And Davood talked about sweeping eyebrows canopying over the sleepy eyes of an angel. That was the substance of what the three of us talked about in that dingy, depressing, three-bed room.

The nurses would rush into our room on time, administer our shots in our butts, give us our pills, and leave. Our talk dissipated one afternoon when a nurse opened the door and came into our room. It was the first time I had ever seen her. She just stood there in the doorway, smiling and looking at us. Mirza and I froze like deer in the headlights for quite a long pause, when finally, she softly moved her lips and said, "I'm here from the social worker's office. I need your names and home addresses so that I can let your families know that you're here." We all exhaled with relief when we realized that this was not our angel. We talked less about her after this incident.

We all realized we were in competition over her and the contest was on as to who would get on his feet sooner and be able to walk to the end of the hallway on the first floor to see her. We got this information out of that heavyset nurse, who unlike the other nurses, was relaxed and personable. She would come into our room three times a day rolling in like a steamroller, pulling along her four-wheel cart of medicines. She would try to act nice and softly ask us to turn over, and administer our shots one by one in our buttocks. Sometimes she would take an extra long time to give the shot. She would find the right spot with her fingers to give the shot; she said it might abscess otherwise. When she would leave, we would wonder why she made it take so long. The veins in Mirza's neck would pop out as he remarked, "Does giving a shot have to take that long?!!"

But none of us said anything to the nurse, for we knew that she was the only person from whom we could gather news about our angel. We gradually got the information out of her by talking about the war, the injured, and the war marches that they would broadcast along with our angel's voice over the loudspeaker. The nurse simply told us that the information booth of the hospital was on the first floor. Once she laughed and asked teasingly why we wanted to know so much about that voice. We panicked and changed the subject and never asked her about it again.

When we found out where she was, our secret competition began, as to which one of us would reach her sooner. Davood was able to walk, but he wouldn't be able to see until his bandages were removed from his eyes. So we were ahead. But with his legs like that, Mirza was not yet ready to get into a wheelchair and move himself down the hallway, for his legs were not yet healed. The doctors said that there was a little infection where the amputation was done, and so he had to remain in his bed for some time. There was only me left, with my torn stomach and that damn colostomy bag which guided the waste into a plastic container that sometimes let out a sound. Davood and Mirza would laugh out loud. We soon called a ceasefire, and became the three friends that we had been in war times cracking jokes in our bunker, the way we had been in happier times in our youth.

I had to win this competition. That's why that day, I waited until I heard her voice on the loudspeaker and I was sure she was still there. It was in the evening on a cold day. The wind was blowing hard outside the windows that until that day, none of us had looked out of. I told Davood and Mirza that I wanted to go out for a walk. At first they were surprised until they realized what my purpose was. Davood smiled vaguely and Mirza looked at me sternly and said that the doctor had forbidden any of us to get out of our beds and that it was not necessary for me to walk. I told him that I wanted to do this, and that it was none of anybody's business, and that I would take full responsibility for my own actions.

I sat up slowly. The pain twisted in my stomach. The colostomy tube felt like a butcher's knife turning inside my intestines. I gripped the edge of the bed and got onto my feet without looking at Davood and Mirza. I held onto the walls as I walked towards the door. I peeked out of my room into the hallway, which was full of incoming injured men. I knew they would stop me if they saw me, and the nurse on shift would take me by the hand and scold me softly and lead me back to bed.

I huddled on the floor amongst the beds and the wounded. I passed by the nurses station. I had only seen this area on the first day I arrived, but I remembered that there were some stairs there that would take me to the first floor. The heavyset nurse was spread out at her desk writing something. Two or three others were sitting beyond her, talking. I waited until the heavyset nurse rose and went to the back. I tiptoed over to the stairs. I was about to walk down the stairs when suddenly my colostomy tube pulled out, and my stomach was twisting in pain. I thought my intestines were going to come out through the wound in my stomach. I had to sit down right there. My face was suddenly wet with perspiration. I was going to go back. I knew I wouldn't be able to make it any further. But then her voice came over the loudspeaker, and when I heard it, I was able to go on. I got up and grabbed onto the green railing and slowly started walking. Her voice was pulling me towards her.

The first floor was crowded with people. Nurses were running to and fro, and hoards of people were waiting behind the glass doors holding pieces of paper with the names of their loved ones written on them. They were fathers and mothers and friends and acquaintances looking for their lost ones. I was heedless as they called out the names to me, asking whether I knew them. I went toward the little glass enclosed information room. She was inside there, behind the frosted glass wall.

With the colostomy bag in hand, I stood there bent over with the worst back pain I had ever experienced. I was exhausted and helpless. I had reached the place I had intended to. I could see the faint shadow of the microphone in front of her through the frosted glass. My heart was pounding and I was wet with perspiration. I wanted to go forward, but couldn't do it. My angel was behind that glass.

It was that image of the angel that had lived in my thoughts and imagination that forced me to get up from my spot and go to her. The irony was that I found myself unable to go any further or see her. She belonged in the imagination of us three friends. Besides, it wasn't becoming of a soldier for me to see her, with Mirza not able to walk and Davood not able to see, languishing behind. All three of us had come out of hell and experienced life and death together. I couldn't jeopardize my experience and our soldier comradery in this slaughterhouse-called-a-hospital and carry the burden of that selfishness around on my shoulders for the rest of my life.

I turned around. It didn't matter now if the nurses saw me or not. But how could I tell them that I went all the way there but wasn't able to go forward and say hello to her? And for Mirza who I knew was eagerly expecting to hear about her, whenever the voice of the angel was broadcast over the loudspeaker, he would stare out the window in ecstasy and smile wistfully. When I opened the door of our room. They both turned to look at me. Maybe it was Mirza or Davood who said, "Aha...."

My body was dripping with perspiration. I was exhausted. I had gone down two flights of stairs and made it back up again with my torn stomach and the damn colostomy tube ripped out. When I lay back down on the bed, Mirza turned to me and asked, "What happened?"

I didn't know what to say. I was stuck. They were both waiting attentively when I answered, "A mermaid."

Mirza blushed and Davood stretched out on the bed. The next day, Mirza got a wheelchair. He climbed carefully down off his bed and told us he was going out to the hallway for a breath of fresh air. All three of us knew where he would be going. He left and we waited until we heard his wheelchair in the hallway. He rolled in, climbed up on the bed, and pulled the sheet up over his face. We had no idea what was the matter. We waited until he calmed down for him to tell us about her. When he was calm, he lifted the sheet and asked me sorrowfully, "Did you see her? Were you able to see at her?" What could I say to him? Or to Davood, who couldn't see anything? Little by little we were starting to accept the bitter fact that all of the doctors hopes were in vain.

After that, the subject came up and we spoke of her again. Mostly we talked to Davood. More than anything, we were waiting for his eyes to get well, and for him to open them, and for us all to see our angel together. But we never got our wish. The next week, the war flared up at the war front and there was a shortage of beds for the seriously wounded – so they discharged us all from the hospital.

Mirza would walk on two artificial legs for the rest of his life. My colostomy bag was soon removed. Davood still thinks that our angel has sweeping brows canopying over big, sleepy, brown eyes, for he will never see again.

2002

A VITAL KILLING

Greetings Mr. Reza Jabbarzadeh, I hope that you are well, considering the circumstances. I am Faramarz Bonkdar. I don't know if you recall my name or not, but I know you and have met you. Of course, this acquaintance goes back to several funeral ceremonies that I attended. You stood by the entrance wearing a black neck scarf and welcomed all who attended. I learned your first name from that funeral invitation.

By the way, on the fortieth day ceremony, I arrived at the graves of the martyrs sooner than you did. I knew where Mohsen's grave was because ever since the day I went on leave, it was a place I had gone many, many times before to see Mohsen, my coach, my battle buddy.

Whenever I would visit him, my throat would tighten and lock up and cause me to gasp for air. People would think I was crazy when I would open my mouth so wide to keep my airways open and breathe. Perhaps they thought I was one of those injured during the recent chemical bombings, especially since my eyes were tearing up so much. Of course, perhaps you may think that these words have really nothing to do with you, and perhaps you are somewhat confused. But when I tell you the rest of the story, you will surely understand my purpose.

That day at the Martyr's Graves, I waited until you arrived with the other mourners. I'm sure you recall sitting in that red Paykan with the black scarf around your neck. The men were in two lines and they started to pound their chests as the procession advanced. The women were walking in line behind the men. You walked until you reached Mohsen's grave. I was standing under the acacia tree by the dirt road across from the grave site. I don't know why I dared not approach you. I felt guilty. I was too ashamed to face you even though you didn't even know who I was. How would you react if you knew that I was forced to kill your son? Yes. Mohsen was murdered by me, not by the enemy soldiers.

I must beg you to please continue reading to the end of this letter and hold judgment until that time. That day, I finally convinced myself to come forward and stand amongst the other mourners, but it was very difficult for me. I tried to hide myself among the other people dressed in black, even though I knew they didn't know me or even my name. But there was a hidden fear that had risen up within me. This fear, along with my guilty conscience was destroying me. I wanted to see you and I wanted to see his mother. You wiped your tears with the corner of your black scarf, and Mohsen's mother, the mother of my coach and battle buddy, had fallen onto his grave and was screaming and calling down hell's damnation upon her son's murder or murders. Imagine the pain and guilt of having killed someone and seeing his family in such anguish.

It was a murder that was done out of necessity and not out of choice. Yes, it was done out of necessity and deliberately. I cannot deny that it was done on purpose. It was I who took your son's life on the night of the operation, but I was forced to do it. And I will tell you the whole story.

I made the decision to explain everything to you from that moment when your son's friend, who was also my battle buddy, took the loudspeaker in his hand to talk about Mohsen. Everything he said was the truth, except about the way your son died. He did not tell you the whole truth. This letter will hopefully make up for that shortcoming.

Your son's friend saw me in the crowd the moment he stepped up to the loudspeaker. His eyes even met my eyes for a few moments. It was for that reason that as he came closer to the end of his talk about his memories of the incident, which led to the martyrdom of your son Mohsen, he raised his head less and less to address the audience and me. You must remember how crushed he was by the end of his talk. He had a wound on his left cheek. As he wiped his tears, the wound opened and started to bleed. You gave your black scarf to him to keep the blood from dripping onto his clothing. And he ended his eulogy there.

Now I would like to tell you the truth about how Mohsen was martyred. That night after sunset, we went into the water – Mohsen, the detachment scuba forces and myself. We were to carry out a siege on the enemy position, which according the map, was next to the Arvand River. While we were trying to get a foothold, which is a military expression that is not necessary to describe, the ready forces on the friendly banks of the river were advancing in boats in order to penetrate the enemy soil.

Like they later told us, the enemy had become suspicious right at the start of the operation about our intention to attack. So after our entry into the waterway, they started firing on the Arvand River. We were all advancing hand-in-hand. Mohsen's left hand was in my right hand. Halfway across the river, the enemy fire became so heavy that we felt like we had fallen into a pot of boiling water. Of course, they had not yet seen us; they were taking shots in the dark. A little further on, we saw some dark objects floating on the water, moving downstream on the Arvand River toward the Persian Gulf. I paid close attention and saw the bodies of scuba forces that belonged to the detachment that was operating to the north of us. Perhaps these details don't matter much to you, but I believe it is my duty to relay every incident that happened that night. Of course, please bear with me and understand why I am not getting straight to the point.

We were about three or four hundred meters away from the enemy shores when your son let out a short scream and started struggling for air like a fish out of water. He was hit in the enemy rain fire. I grabbed him under his arms so that I wouldn't lose him in the dark of night. With all of the weapons and ammunitions on his back, he might have sunk under the water and we would have been deprived of ever seeing him again. Your son's friend said that Mohsen was martyred in the water, and the commander of our scuba detachment ordered someone else by the name of Bonkdar to take Mohsen's body to the enemy shore so that he would not be lost. Perhaps by now you remember my name. But Mohsen was still alive then, even though he would not have survived that wound. Our commander ordered us to get Mohsen to shore by a line of scuba divers. Then enemy fire subsided and I was able to take off Mohsen's and my weapons and equipment and leave them in the water so that I could carry him more easily to shore. He had taken a bullet to the neck. I put my arm around his waist and swam with him. In those moments, all of my thoughts were for saving Mohsen's life, especially because he had once saved mine. I held his head up such that the waves would not obstruct his breathing. This was possible to do and in that three or four hundred meters that I swam, I did this to the best of my ability.

We reached the enemy shores. We were blocked by barbed wires, floating anti-ship barriers, bamboo stalks and reeds. The enemy soldiers who were standing guard did not see us when we reached the shores where we waited and rested behind the barbed wire. Our commander radioed us from the operations headquarters and ordered us to wait until more troops arrived at the rendezvous point. This was when the gurgling sound in Mohsen's throat started.

Air was passing through the bullet hole making a lot of noise. The commander of our detachment swam over to my side and told me to cut his noise. I changed Mohsen's position this way and that, hoping to stop the noise coming from his throat. But I couldn't. At this point, I saw one of the enemy soldiers who went up to the observation post above the bunkers to look out. He was suspicious. I prayed a thousand times that prayer they say to deafen the enemy ear. The commander came back and this time vehemently ordered me to cut his noise. I didn't understand what he meant by that. I said helplessly, "I've done whatever I could but it won't stop." The commander told me once more to stop his noise. I asked how. He said to put his head under the water. I couldn't believe what I had heard at first, but as he stayed there staring at me in solemn silence, I realized he was serious. That noise kept coming from my coach and your son, Mohsen's throat. Waves would hit us, and the water would go into his throat and spout out like a fountain. And that is what led me to take Mohsen by the wrists and pull him under the water, even though he was unconscious above the water. As soon as I took his head under the water, he moved and grabbed something and pulled himself up. Our commander was by our side, and again angrily ordered me to pull him under, and emphasized that if our position was found out, all of our forces would be jeopardized. I grabbed both of Mohsen's arms from above and below the shoulder blades, took a deep breath, and pulled him under the water. It was very difficult for me. My six-month acquaintance with Mohsen passed before my eyes moment by moment.

The day the forces were being divided up, I passed myself off as an expert swimmer and joined the scuba squadron. They took us to the Karoon River. Your Mohsen, my scuba coach, stood before us and told us that we must be able to swim across the river and back, but that on the first day, we would only be required to jump in and tread water to demonstrate our level of expertise. I panicked. There was no other choice. Your son ordered everybody all at once into the water. I didn't think it would be very deep, but when I couldn't feel anything under my feet, I felt death was at hand. I struggled in the water and swallowed a lot of water. But when I opened my eyes, I was on the shores and saw Mohsen pressing on my chest with his two hands. I was alive. Your son had rescued me and pulled me out of the water.

We soon got to know each other so well that we even knew each other's most private secrets. Yes, six months of friendship passed before my eyes in less than one minute. I couldn't stand seeing Mohsen, who had saved my life, struggle like that while I held him under the water, depriving him of his life. This time it was I who pulled him up to the surface and raised his head out of the water before my own, so that my battle buddy and my coach and friend could breathe.

Our commander had advanced forward. As soon as the sound of Mohsen's gurgling throat reached his ears, he came back over to us quickly. Outside the water it was absolute silence. But under the water, it felt like I was in the middle of a heavy storm of sounds that were blasting my ear drums. Our commander whispered in my ear; it was a whisper that as hushed as it was, had the intensity of shouting in my ear as the commander said, "Don't you realize where we are? If we are found out they will decimate us! Not only us, but the other forces too." Mohsen's throat was getting louder moment by moment. I told him, "I can't do it." Our commander looked at me there in the dark. He was thinking that I meant I couldn't do it in a physical sense. He said, "Then I'll help you."

I was resigned. I tried to not to think of anything, not of our past, or of my life that he had saved, or our friendship and comradery, and not even you, his father, who I would surely have to face in the future. The commander ordered me to hold his head and he grabbed Mohsen's two feet. Together we went under the water. At first, Mohsen didn't move, but then he started to struggle, kick and flail his arms. He kicked our commander back and his face got caught on the barbed wire. Of course, I realized this later when Mohsen stopped struggling and we all surfaced. We latched your son's corpse onto the barbed wire so that the tide would not carry him out to sea. Your son looked like Christ crucified amongst the thorns, his arms outstretched and his head fallen sideways onto his chest.

Our commander wiped the blood from his left cheek with the sleeve of your son's scuba diving suit. Then he ordered us to attack. And I never saw Mohsen again.

This is the whole truth about what happened to your son. I told it to you in all candidness. Now I am prepared to accept any punishment that you and your family wish for me. I murdered Mohsen and I must bear the consequences of that. Whatever you decide, I will accept. You can find me in that same squadron that your son was in. The address is on the back of this envelope. And now I leave you because I know that you need solitude. Please know that I am also grieving for your late only son, my friend and comrade, Mohsen.

Faramarz Bonkdar

1999

THE RETURN

Our company was gathered by the tracks waiting for the train that was to take us veteran, volunteer soldiers back to our homes and cities after the end of the war. It was hot, very hot. It was sunset when they told us to line up behind the barbed wire and go through an inspection.

They scattered all of our belongings on the ground, though we had nothing but old, dirty clothes and worn, faded boots, an old parachute from our maneuvers and a few empty shells from the shots that we had fired. These were the only spoils of our youth spent in the war.

Our Long John Silver who had one eye, had always said since the beginning that he was going to take his bayonet home with him. And that was how when it came to his turn we watched the inspector with the red hat from the other side of the barbed wire fence to see what he would do. He took out Long John's clothes and things one by one. There was a yellow t-shirt, and dirty pants that only had one leg. He felt around inside the bag and pulled out the bayonet. That inspector with the red hat put back his spear and said calmly, "Thank God this is the last time we see him, otherwise I would...."

When Long John came out, we sat down outside the barbed wire.

Our commander gathered the fifteen of us around him. His dirty sleeves were frayed. He had crawled five kilometers in this last attack with a wounded leg. He was still limping and was thin, gaunt and sunburnt. His hair and beard were tangled and dirty. He sternly told us to sit down but not in the sense of giving us an order, for he no longer technically had any authority over us. But we didn't want to end on a different note with him or for him to think we no longer thought of him as our commander. He put his hand on his hip and said calmly, "Well, this is the last day of the war. When we arrive home, people will come and greet us. They will have many lambs and cattle ready to sacrifice and they will have bought up all the flowers in the flower shops. They will have put all of their effort into this final homecoming to make it a glorious one for all of you who are the pride of our religion and country." Then he gave an "at ease" order and we all relaxed and sat down on the ground. Conversations blossomed. We were all excited about what we would be doing after the war. Some of them wanted to pursue their studies. Some would pursue employment and a simple life. But most of us hadn't a clue about what to do next.

We were just getting to the interesting parts of our conversations when Long John, who had been listening with his ear on the rail, called out, "It's here! It's here!"

A wave overtook the group of us waiting there. We all got up and looked down the tracks with our hands shading our eyes from the sun. The train was chugging along, as it got nearer. Some people ran down the tracks and pushed others out of the way where the train was to stop. People cleared the way, picking up their backpacks and hanging them over their backs as we all waited for the train to stop, so we would be ready to pour into train quickly as it stopped, and be first to get a seat. Long John ordered, "Get three cabins, three of them! We're staying up all night!"

The train came quickly without slowing down, and all we saw were people on the other side of the windows gawking at the sea of people outside. Some of them smiled and some other ones waved.

We sat back down. The sun was setting. Maybe that's why we stopped talking. We sat hugging our knees staring at each other and saw our past in each other. All we had seen was war, night battles, joking and laughing with one another throughout our early and late youth. One of them yelled, "The train! The train is here!"

A few people moved to the middle of the crowd and opened the way again where the train would stop, and we'd quickly hop on and get to our cities where they were waiting for us.

The train labored as it moved toward us and separated the crowds as it rattled right on by.

We went back to our places again, and this time Reza took out a red notebook and gave it to us to write down our addresses, so that later we could visit each other in the days after the war. That spurred the others to take out pieces of paper to collect names and addresses on as well, as the third train came and left without anyone moving from his spot.

The sun went down. We wanted to go back to the other side of the barbed wire fence so that we could perform our evening prayers, but they wouldn't let us back in and said that our slips had already had been stamped as exited, and in that case we wouldn't be allowed back in. All they did was feed a garden hose through the barbed wire fence to provide us some water.

It was now dark. We talked through the dark night, about the past and the people who were martyred in the final moments of the war. We were mourning for Reza, the youngest volunteer warrior in our midst. If he had only lived a few more days, he would now be here with us. Then one by one, we picked up our backpacks and tucked them under our heads as pillows for the night. The clamor of the guys on both sides of the rail subsided. Nobody watched for the trains that were coming from the south, destined for the cities in the central part of the country. Everybody knew that they would not stop to pick us up.

The soldiers went to sleep. Sounds rose up amongst the groggy or sleepless ones. Every so often one who was still awake would shout, "The train is here!" and when we would open our eyes, we would see people in the flickering light of the rapidly passing train, sitting up straight looking out at us with their faces pressed to the glass. This was our situation all night until someone yelled, "Morning prayers!"

It was morning. The sun had risen. People were irritable. We were stuck there and nobody was paying any attention to us. It was as if we had been completely forgotten. It was then when the commander of our company yelled, "That's enough! They've kept us here since yesterday and they keep saying they're going to send a train! We don't need a big welcome or flowers! Our wives and children and mothers and fathers are waiting for us....and after all these years!" And we knew well that he was dying to see his only daughter, Roya. We knew this because when the rubber would hit the road in the crucial times during the war, he would take out his daughter's photo, look at it and kiss it. We would try to steal a peek, but we could never see anything. After that, the guys started yelling. Everybody started saying something. One of them raised the commander up on his shoulders and the commander continued, "There are only fifteen soldiers remaining in our company since last year. We cannot tolerate this situation anymore. If they don't send a train to take us home soon, we will stop a train in its tracks and force them to take us home."

The company gathered on the rails. Nobody said a word. They were all looking down the tracks. The train looked like a wounded snake as it came slithering, sliding and twisting down the tracks in the horizon. We didn't move from our spots. The train blew its whistle as it got nearer. It came to a stop directly in front of the first person in our line. And that was when we all hopped on.

Long John broke the glass with his cane, and the commander tore off the door. Reza went over someone's shoulders and jumped on. The sound of windows smashing was everywhere. We were uncontrollable. The train filled up with us old, volunteer soldiers. We forced people out of their cabins and sat down in their places. But still the train did not move. We were sweating profusely, but happy.

Then when they said that our commander had spoken to the train conductor, and the two had agreed that the soldiers would give back the cabins and be allowed to sit in the aisles, everything ended harmoniously.

The commander of our company gathered us around outside of the cabins in the halls. We sat lined up single file. He said sternly, "Never mind, just bear it one more day." We were sitting there hugging our knees among the baggage - isolated in the space between two passenger cars. The train started to move. There was complete silence, except for the sound of the rattling train. We were drowning in our thoughts of ourselves, our past, the present, our future.

The conductor in the blue uniform came into our car and stood over us. He looked at us for a few moments and then yelled, "Hey! Why are you all sitting here blocking the way? People need to pass through here to get to the bathroom!"

We all got up but didn't know where to go.

2001

THE DEAD END

Mr. interrogator, sir, I have already told you everything in the interview. It's all in your interrogation notes. And I've already provided a written statement about these two suicides.

Well, Amir Hossein and Maryam were my grandchildren. I was home that night when this happened. I had gone to the 21st Night Ceremony at the mosque, the same mosque where I pray every night. They were both fasting. We had our fast-breaking meal that evening after dusk, and then I left. I don't know what time it was, but I came back and saw them both on the floor in the middle of the room. They had died from gas asphyxiation. Only God knows how they came up with that plan. I had heard them tell me a long time ago about a person who had killed himself this way. I can't remember whether it was some dignitary or a writer. I can't think anymore, let alone remember names.

Yes, I'll tell you from the very beginning. Whenever you need me to elaborate further just let me know. Well, where should I begin? I'll start from the time when our household was hit by this curse. It was during the days of the uprisings when my wife died. I had just retired and bought a house on this dead end street where I am presently living. I had just retired. I already told you, I was in the military. I was an officer in the gendarmerie and served my country for thirty years with honor. I was the head of the police headquarters in Esfahan, Shahr Kurd, Yasooj and Khuzestan. When I retired, I came back here. Yes, yes, I was saying that my wife died during those turbulent times. It was the 7th of September. She had gone to a protest demonstration. You must have heard about them. You don't seem old enough to have experienced those times. Jaleh was caught up in the killing in the middle of the square. Yes, she came home and said that she was in that crowd of people. That night, she had a heart attack and died. Yes, I heard it myself. Now some people say that Sam and Nariman's mother killed herself. They were just lies that people were whispering. No sir, I was retired and had come back here. No sir, interrogator, she had slept well that night, but in the morning did not wake up. The doctors said that the reason for her death was a heart attack.

Well, at that time, the kids were grown. We only had our two boys. Sam was three or four years older than Nariman. They started supporting the revolution around that time, going to the protest

86

marches every day. They never stopped going even though their mother had suffered a heart attack. Later on, they took up arms and stood guard in the streets. Well, what do I know, sir? That was when Mitra came along. I wasn't happy about it at all. He came and said that he wanted to marry one of the believing "sisters". I said, "Young man! Does a person marry his own sister?!" You know, people used to talk like that in those days. He wasn't having any of that. He made himself clear that he wanted her. When I gave in, he said he wanted to hold his wedding ceremony inside the mosque. I said, "Come on, be logical! The mosque is a place for funerals and mourning, not for weddings!" He wasn't having any of that. He invited his friends. No one came from the family. Can you believe that, Mr. interrogator? People in our family still ridicule me over this very subject. Forget it. As I was saying, some of his friends came, as he called them, "sisters and brothers". Both of them were wearing that Islamic garb and they were each holding an M-1 rifle. No, I tore up all their photos. After Mitra died, I didn't ever want to see them again.

I brought them home myself. You came there. It was that same room by the door. I cleared it out and let them live there. They spread out one of those military blankets in the middle of the room and started their married life there with four books and two outfits of clothing. I left them to themselves. I pretended that they didn't even live there. You're no stranger here. I didn't even answer Mitra when she would say hello.

Nariman was just the opposite of Sam. No sir, he was nothing like that. Sam really wanted to pull Nariman into the cause, but Nariman wouldn't have it. He turned to his studies and lessons. He would not associate much with Sam. When the war started, Sam went to the war front. After he returned, he went back for a second deployment. Amir Hossein was born right around then. I don't remember exactly what month and day. Can't you look at his birth certificate?

Sam was at the front when he was born. To tell you the truth, I didn't even want to drive that girl Mitra to the hospital. Sam was my son. He had caused me enough trouble, let alone a grandson.

When the war started, my other son Nariman got serious about his studies. He wanted to go to college and be exempted from military service at any cost. If he had not gone to college, they would have drafted him into the military. And being in the military in a time of war, you know better what that is like.

I think it was the year 1361 when they announced they were going to take back the city of Khorramshahr in an attack. You remember that? Like these so-called sisters and brothers, at that time, Khorramshahr was called "Khooninshahr" – "Flourishing City" had turned into "Bloody City". Yes, well, I was there for two years at the end of my service, at the Khein Headquarters, right near Khorramshahr. We would go to that city at night, to the banks of the Karoon River, by the bridge next to the Shatt al-Arab. We had some good times there, sir.

They started broadcasting war marches on the radio. After that, thousands of bodies were brought home from the war front. There were memorial shrines set up on almost every street in the neighborhoods. This daughter-in-law of mine, Mitra, was jumping up and down like popcorn when the military officials came. There were three of them, two women and one man. Well, it was obvious why they were there. Everybody already knew. They came into the living room and sat down. At first, one of the women said a few things, and then the man spoke about their detachment had advanced too far at the border and they were all mass murdered. They had not been able to retrieve the bodies and bring them back.

The officials had barely left the house when the "brothers" came into our alley and strung up lights and decorated with flags. You see sir, what days we're living in? Everything is the opposite! He got married in the mosque where they pray for the dead and pass out dates at funerals! And they decorated our alley and passed out cold drinks at his funeral!

A few days later, they brought a street sign and posted it at the entrance to our alley. They named our alley, Martyr Sam Alley. I went several times to reason with them. I told them, sir, I was in the military. I know that area. I pleaded with them to at least let me go and bring back my son's body myself. But they wouldn't allow it. Well, then after that, there was nothing more I could do. People's attitudes had changed. I would go to the mosque at sunset, perform my prayers, and go straight home.

After a year had passed since Sam's death, the prayer leader at our mosque asked to speak with me. He told me that Sam's wife should not remain a widow forever, and things like that. I'm sure you know what I mean. Then he suggested that the martyr's brother would be able to take care of this woman and her son best of all. At first, I wasn't in agreement with him, but when I thought more about it, I thought that at least my grandson would not eventually fall into the custody of a bad stepfather. They spoke with Nariman. That was how Nariman and Mitra got married. I think it was September the following year when Maryam was born. Nariman was exempted from military service because of Sam. The next year, he went to the university on a special grant. He soon achieved a high ranking and became the head of a company. Mr. interrogator, Nariman was not like Sam at all. He was a very clever boy. It is so sad. What a waste. What a waste.

Well, it was in 1990 when they announced that the POWs would be freed. It had been two years since the war ended. One night when I was on my way home from the mosque after dark, saw some women in our alley gathered around, whispering. As I passed, they became quiet, but no one said anything to me. Perhaps Mitra and Nariman knew about it, and was why they didn't come out of their room for two or three days.

90

They informed us that Sam had indeed been a prisoner of war and would be freed soon. I was in shock. I didn't know what to do. Nobody offered any suggestions. It was exactly on the night of the 16th of October when he returned. He had become thin and grey haired, and his hands shook like someone with Parkinson's disease. People gathered at the entrance to our alleyway. Nobody thought to take down our street sign. When Sam got out of the car, he said hello to everyone. They all chanted blessings all the way to our gate, but nobody came in. It's like they wanted to deliver him home and escape. And that's exactly what they did. Yes, yes, I'll tell you.

We all sat down in the living room together. Poor Nariman and that girl Mitra! Their heads were lowered. Sam sat Amir Hossein on one of his legs and Maryam on the other leg. Amir Hossein was probably eight years old, and Maryam, five. Sam started to pat their heads. Well, he had been away from his country and his son for many years. Then he asked whose daughter this is. Amir Hossein blurted out that she was his sister. Mitra nervously interrupted him and said to Sam, "She is your brother Nariman's daughter." When he heard this, Sam started to kiss her and taking in her scent, and telling his brother congratulations, and asking about his wife, and things like that. Believe me, dear Mr. interrogator, even if Sam had not killed Nariman, Nariman himself would have died in anguish. Mitra too. You should have seen their faces. They all as pale as the dead.

Well, I had to tell him what happened somehow. I told him how they informed our family that he had been martyred, and the rest of the story. There was nothing we could do. He had to know sooner or later. If I hadn't told him, some one else would have.

Well, the rest of the story that I've told you before does not need to be repeated. I want to get this over with and move on to the subject of the suicides of Amir Hossein and Maryam. Well, yes, if I must give you a statement, I will.

Sam didn't say anything at first. He just stared at me. He must have felt like he was about to die. He sat there staring at me, Amir Hossein and Maryam, and Nariman and Mitra for almost an hour. His face was so scary that Amir Hossein was frightened and clung to his mother. Then Sam got up and went into the kitchen. He came back in with a cleaver in his hands. I wasn't sure what he was going to do. He went and fell down onto Nariman and stabbed him with the knife – not once but five times. Everything is there in the coroner's report. Mitra was screaming and Amir Hossein was bawling and by the time I was able to grab the wall and pull myself up, everything was over. He had cut Nariman's head completely off and left the house. Yes, the officers came and took away the body. They were looking for Sam's picture. They were looking through the photo albums for his picture before his captivity, asked a few questions and left. They said they would come back the next day. That night, Mitra killed herself. Her body was found in her room. The next morning Amir Hossein came to me and told me that his mother would not wake up. She was on the floor in the middle of the room. The autopsy revealed that she had killed herself by taking a handful of pills.

I was left with this little boy and girl. I decided to raise them to remember my children. After a few days, I noticed they had painted over my son's name on our street sign. No, they did not take it down. They just painted over it.

Little by little, people started talking and whispering, and I knew what they were saying about Amir Hossein and Maryam. The children soon also found out. Eventually, they didn't want to go out to the alley to play anymore. When they came home, they would stay in their room.

No sir, interrogator, we never talked about the past. We never mentioned the names Sam, Nariman or Mitra. These names were like forbidden fruit. Amir Hossein was twenty, and Mitra, seventeen years old. Mr. interrogator, I don't know how this misfortune fell upon our household.

It was in the middle of the night when I came back from the ceremony at the mosque. As soon as I turned the key and opened the front door, I could smell gas fumes. I did not turn on the light. I opened all the doors and turned off the gas main. When I finally turned on the lights, I saw that they had purposefully disconnected the gas line from the heater. They were in their room. I went inside and saw their bodies sprawled out on the floor.

Yes sir, interrogator. I'm at home. I'm going to leave at sunset to visit the cemetery. Today is the twenty-fifth anniversary of my wife's death. I'll be back soon. You may come and see me then. You are welcome to come then. The door to their room is unlocked. There are just a few books and things in there. If I'm not here when you arrive, the neighbors will have a key. You can open the door and go on inside.

Ok, so where should I sign?

2004

THE GIFT

Our commander said we were going to do a drawing. We all agreed, but when he pulled out the matchsticks, we all reneged.

The five of us sat against the walls of the group bunker that we had all built together before the grand operation. It was sunset. The bleary rays of sunlight filtered through the fanned-out date palm leaves into the three corners of our bunker.

We were all quiet. We knew that the drawing would fall upon one of us, who would have to carry out the mission. None of us wanted it.

The commander showed each one of us the five matchsticks, and then broke one of them in half. He held the matchsticks behind his head, paused, and then brought them back out in front of him. He looked at us seriously as he held out the five pink matchstick heads between his two fingers. He said gently, "Pull one."

We each had to pull one to determine whom the mission would fall upon to carry out. None of us dared offer to take one first. We stood there in a daze, looking at the pink matchstick heads. Suddenly a bomb fell and exploded next to our bunker and the acrid smell of burned gunpowder seeped through the seams of the sandbag walls and windows.

My throat burned and felt dry. If I waivered, the others would find an excuse and say that I was the best person to carry out the mission, so I extended my hand to pull the first matchstick, when my commander retracted his hand, smiled wryly and said, "Forget about drawing matchsticks. You're going!"

I wanted to say something, but the others were so overjoyed, they didn't give me the chance. They interrupted me and said all together that I had to go, and that the drawing was a mistake from the very beginning.

I walked out of the bunker. The sun was clawing at the leaves of the date palm tree as if it didn't want to go down behind the horizon until it saw what I would do next. I didn't know what I would do. I myself believed that fate had chosen me to go and take the news to Naneh Abdo and receive the gift she had been promising recently to anyone who would bring news about Abdo to her.

I set out through the date palm grove that led to a road that was built by a group of engineers before the first attack. No one followed me out to see me off or to wish me well. When I turned around, I saw them all clinging inside the bunker, watching me through the openings between the sand bags. I walked through Zaer Abbas' date palm grove, where heavy artillery had been installed and large community bunkers had been built. There were soldiers here and there in the date palm grove. Soldiers and scuba divers have passed through here leaving only empty bunkers and mounds of dirt behind.

The smell of burnt gunpowder permeated the Zaer Abbas date palm grove. Now, the buffalo are no longer scattered everywhere, and Abdo's voice is no longer heard here amongst the trees, as he throws his buffalo at the Bahman Shir River.

I hit a detour in the road. Several heavy artillery shells explode in the distance. A whipping sound passes over my head, and then it is silent everywhere. I hear the faint sound of soldiers yelling. The sound is coming from the direction of Bahman Shir. For sure they have found a wild boar left behind, and tracked it to hunt it and take the edge off their hunger pangs like they always do. They take off any time of day or night to go after wild boar in the outskirts of the Dashtban River groves. They try to hunt the wild boar itself, but if not, they capture its young. They build a campfire and then the partying begins with smells of barbeque filling the air.

In the morning we would pack up our net tents on our backs, and follow Abdo's father. We would board the boat and hit the water, passing the Bahman Shir to the Arvand River where we would throw our nets into the water. Zaer Ibrahim would stand over us smoking a cigarette. Abdo and I would be sitting on the floor of the boat, talking quietly until Zaer Ibrahim would call us to pull the net out of the water. We would then go back at sunset. Zaer Ibrahim would give us our share and Abdo and I would run back to Chooibdeh, which back then was a village of only about 10 to 15 mud brick houses. We would sell the fish and buy cigarettes. Then we'd walk around the date palm grove smoking our cigarettes and taking the long way home.

That was where one day Zaer Ibrahim hit the water and Abdo saw him yelling, "Shark! Shark!"

The fin above the water was a shark circling Zaer Ibrahim seven times. Then the waters of the Bahman Shir became turbulent and took on the color of blood. The men ran, got onto their boats and hit the water. They raised up their daggers in their hands and beat them down into the water and pulled Zaer Ibrahim out of the water, half alive. His right leg was bitten off above the knee.

I turn toward Zaer Ibrahim's date palm grove. Now all of the cabins and mud brick houses in the date palm grove have been turned into military station stables and even though much of the military has left here since the great attack, their forces are still lingering inside the date palm grove to get everything dismantled.

Before the great attack, they ordered people out of their homes, saying that staying there was too dangerous. Only Zaer Ibrahim and Naneh Abdo stayed. No matter how much the commander of the operations insisted that non-military elements must vacate the area, they kept saying that they had nowhere else to go. No matter how the military assured them that they would be given a tent behind the front line, Naneh Abdo stood by her word, "A person who has a home does not sleep in a tent."

The military didn't know why they were so adamant about staying, but we understood that they weren't going to leave Abdo behind and go elsewhere. And now that destiny had entrusted me with the task of bringing them this news, I don't know whether they will still remain there or not.

It has been more than three months since they have brought the forces and equipment here. We two were of the scouts. Before the war, we had crossed the Arvand many times and in these three months, had become the scout of the commanders and the reconnaissance groups. We would put on scuba suits every night and take them forward by way of the safe route, which was our childhood playground and secret hiding place where we smoked cigarettes.

The night of the attack, a squad of reconnaissance scuba divers was sent out ahead. Were two scout were heading up that squad.

Wherever you set eyes in the dark under the moonlight, you would see columns of hundreds of scuba divers in black suits headed toward the western banks of the river. We were in the middle of the river when the sky lit up as light as day. We panicked as to what it could be. We started to panic when the machine guns started firing without cease. Right there in the middle of the river, Abdo was hit by a bullet, and it was such bedlam that they gave orders for the living to return to shore. I looked for him, but I couldn't locate him among so many bodies floating gently toward the sea. They all looked the same floating lifelessly in black scuba suits.

I went back. I returned to shore. There were only a few of us left from among all those scuba divers. The soldiers on the other side had unceasingly fired upon the river and ramified with artillery until bodies began floating calmly toward the sea.

We went back to our bunkers. At first light, our commander ordered us to set out for the mouth of the Persian Gulf. We didn't know why. We all piled into the back of an open pickup truck and started out before sunrise. When we got there, we saw that they had spread hundreds of fishing nets over the water. We hopped off the trucks and got onto motor boats and small fishing boats as they sent us after the nets. They ordered us to pull up the nets. It just now dawned on us that our mission was fishing for dead bodies.

We pulled up the nets into the boats, threw the live, flapping fish back into the water, and lined up the corpses in scuba suits next to each other. We did this for three days and three nights without rest. I was looking for Abdo. The motor and fishing boats docked one by one next to each other at the shore as they delivered their loads and left. The corpses were laid out next to each other. The trucks came one by one and loaded them up and left. I was by the shore wandering amongst the bodies, waiting for the next boat to arrive in the hopes that maybe Abdo could be found.

When the commanders grew doubtful that any new bodies could be pulled from the water and the nets were being pulled up empty, they ordered us to go back to our old bunkers. The fighting was diminishing and now that we had not been able to besiege the lands on the other side of the river, little by little they pulled back the artillery weapons and the forces.

Zaer Ibrahim and Naneh Abdo had come to the station looking for me and Abdo. I hid myself and the others told them that we were in the bunkers by the Arvand River waiting for fresh forces to replace them before they could come back. The smell of buffalo manure and the cool rotting grass fills my senses. A pile of empty artillery shell casings shone a rusty copper color in the yellow sunlight. As I maneuver around the pile of shell casings, I see Zaer Ibrahim wearing a tunic and walking with a cane as he scatters seed for the chickens. He sees me from afar and waves his cane in the air and yells, "Haaa! Jalal! You've finally come!"

I hop over a dried up stream and say hello. Zaer Ibrahim is scattering moistened bread crumbs in front of the chickens and roosters and says, "These were leftovers from the soldiers' mess hall. They waste so much bread!"

I ask, "Where is Naneh Abdo, Zaer?"

He replies, "She's inside. Go on in. I'll be right there."

"Is she better?" I ask.

He serenely glances up to the skies and says, "Well, she's gotten a lot weaker in the past few days." but stops himself from saying anything more.

I had hid myself inside the bunker. They said that they could hear a wolf howling on the other side of the date palm grove every sunset. I knew that all the artillery fire had caused most of the wildlife in the area, even the wild boar to flee.

Sometimes when Abdo and I were in the mood, we would tease them and chase their young. One day the commander informed me that Zaer Ibrahim had shown up at the station demanding to see his son's best friend, Jalal. It was almost sunset when I arrived.

I could hear the squeals of the wild boar's young left behind in the distance, and the soldiers' shouting and yelling and the sound of the sniper rifles that were so loud. Naneh Abdo was squatting by that other date palm tree. She had hung a rope around her neck with the other end tied to the Afflicted Zainab tree, as Zaer Ibrahim had named it. She came crawling to me on all fours. She turned in a circle and then glared at me like an injured female wolf and howled. The intensity in her eyes frightened me. I looked away at Zaer Ibrahim and saw him kneeling before her with a look of death on his face.

I sat down next to Zaer Ibrahim. She turned in a circle again and looked straight into the sun and howled like she was dying. Zaer Ibrahim simply looked on as Naneh Abdo circled the date palm again and again and again.

I grabbed Zaer Ibrahim and helped him up. We went inside. I asked him what happened. He said that Naneh Abdo knows that something has happened to Abdo, and that they won't tell her anything. She has been in solitude. She had a dream about him and has made this howling pact with God in return for news of her son to reach her within forty days.

While it was light outside, I wasn't able to leave that mud-brick room that smelled of my childhood with Abdo, but when I heard the anguished squeals of the wild boar mixed with the sniper guns, I got out of there. In the distance they were firing artillery, and the date palm grove was on fire.

Zaer Ibrahim moistened more bread in that same bowl he used for the chickens, and placed it before Naneh Abdo and said, "The sun has gone down. Have your evening meal, woman." The howling of the female wolf diminished and she slowly came forward, put her head into the bowl and started devouring the food.

"How are you, Jalal?" Naneh Abdo stands before me hunched over leaning on her cane. I say hello and rush up to greet her.

Naneh Abdo comes forward as I step sideways. "Haa! Have you brought news of Abdo? I had a dream about him."

Every time I went there, these were always Naneh Abdo's same words. "He was different this time. My child was different this time."

Wanting to change the subject, Zaer Ibrahim says, "Ok. Go inside. It's cold out here. I'll be inside as soon as I get the lamp lit."

The room smells musty. Zaer Ibrahim hangs the lamp on a hook on the wall, drops his cane and limps over and sits down against the flower print pillow at the head of the room. Naneh Abdo comes in and goes into the other room. We remain quiet, both Zaer Ibrahim and I.

I came back here again after that time. Naneh Abdo was still on all fours by the tree she had tied herself to that they called the Afflicted Zainab. When it would get dark, her howls would penetrate the date palm grove. I could hear her as far away as the station. At dusk, the firing was lighter and it was quiet everywhere.

People soon found out what the sound of the female wolf howling was. Some people said that when it gets dark, wild roaming boar encircle Zaer Ibrahim's house and when Naneh Abdo starts howling, they join her by squealing. It is a chilling sound. When it would get dark, we would all go find someplace to hide. I would hide in the corner of the bunker with a blanket over my head because I couldn't stand listening to it.

One day, they called me down to the Arvand. They said in code over the CB radio that they had caught a shark and emphasized that I get down there immediately. I got on a motorcycle and rode down there. On the shore, there was a shark laid out on its back with its belly sliced open. One person, bloody from head to toe was walking around with a dagger in his hand. They spilled guts out of the belly of the shark onto the muck and mud on the shore with its nauseating odor. Two people had run their arms up to the elbows reaching into the shark's belly searching for something. I was confused. I didn't know why they had summoned me, and wondered what hunting sharks had to do with me.

I was in this thought when a man approached me with a dagger in hand. He had on an olive colored windbreaker spotted in blood. He put his hand into his pocket, brought out a few pieces of paper and asked me, "This Abdo, son of Zaer Ibrahim, was he your friend? That one whose mother went crazy after losing her son?" I realized that he was a local. I answered him, but he didn't listen to me. He turned to yell at the two people who were looking for a treasure it seemed inside the belly of the shark, "Well, go easy! Look carefully!" Then he reached into a bag he was carrying and took out a bloody plastic bag. He opened it and took out a metal tag. "Was this your friend, Abdo's tag? The number is correct." I grabbed the tag from his hand. The number was correct, AG-325-476. His tag number was only one number different from mine. I reply immediately, "Yeah. It's his. Abdo, son of Zaer Ibrahim. Where was he found? Where is he?" I was confused. Abdo's bloody tag, a shark with its belly split open from head to toe, and men carrying daggers and then those two men searching left what they were doing and walked up to me and told me that just that morning at the mouth of the sea they had caught a shark from which seven tags were found in its belly. One of those was this one. And now I was to undertake the task of giving this news to his parents. It was a mission that fell to me despite the drawing that was to determine who would go.

Naneh Abdo comes back in with the tray of tea, two cups and a sugar bowl decorated with red roses on it. She sits down. She stares into my eyes and I drop my head. "Last night I dreamed about him. I saw him walking on water. I said, Abdo, whoever brings me news of you, I will give him a gift. But you come back instead."

Outside, a nightingale's singing seems near at first and is loud but then it hops and flies away and the chirping grows distant. "Where is Abdo? Have they taken him captive? Is he in the hospital? Don't you have any news of him?"

I want to get up and go back without telling her anything. How will I be able to utter these words? Abdo's news is only one metal tag left behind, which I have brought with me. I begin speaking carefully, measuring my words and then I get agitated and start speaking more quickly and explain to her everything that she needs to know. When I raise my head I see Zaer Ibrahim and Naneh Abdo looking back at me in shock, as if they were both dead in their places. I don't know how long we just sat there looking at each other. Then Naneh Abdo places the cups of tea in front of us and takes the tray away. I put the tag on the tray and she looks at it blankly and gets up. It takes a few moments for her to straighten up. Then then she slowly walks into the next room.

I am sitting there with my head lowered, lost in my thoughts of running away from there when I hear Naneh Abdo's footsteps. She stops in front of me. I don't dare raise my head. "Here you are, Jalal. Here is your gift."

I slowly raise my head and see her standing before me. She holds the tray in front of her as she slowly moves to her knees and sits in front of me. I see two holes in her face with blood gushing down both of her cheeks to her chin, dripping onto her dress. There is a metal tag and two eyes looking up at me longingly from a tray full of blood.

2004

Ahmad Dehghan was born in 1966. He holds a Master's Degree in Anthropology from Tehran University. His first novel, Journey To Heading 270 Degrees was published in 1996. Two years later, this novel was chosen as one of the selections in Twenty Years of Story Writing. Later, this novel was chosen as one of the selections in Twenty Years of Lasting Literature.

He has written scholarly articles in his field of Anthropology, as well as editorials on memoir writing, especially memoir writing on the subject of the Iran-Iraq War.

Ahmad Dehghan's books have been translated into many of the world's languages.

Ahmad Dehghan's works:
>Mission Accomplished
>Moments of Anxiety
>The Final Days
>The Stars of Shalamcheh
>Journey to Heading 270 Degrees
>Four Men Patrol
>Incursion
>A Vital Killing
>The Lookout
>Prowling the Enemy Soil

ABOUT THE TRANSLATOR

Caroline Croskery's interests have been focused on the Persian culture for many years. She was born in the United States and moved to Iran at the age of twenty-one. She holds a Bachelor's Degree from the University of California at Los Angeles in Iranian Studies where she graduated Cum Laude. For many years, she has been active in three fields of specialization: Language Teaching, Translation and Interpretation and Voiceover Acting.

During her thirteen years living in Iran, she taught English and also translated as well as dubbed Iranian feature films into English. After returning to live in the United States, she began a ten-year career as a court interpreter and translator of books from Persian into English. She is an accomplished voiceover talent, and currently continues her voiceover career in both English and Persian.

Other titles translated and narrated by Caroline Croskery are:

Languor of the Morn, by Fattaneh Haj Seyed Javadi
We Are All Sunflowers, by Erfan Nazarahari
Democracy or Democrazy, by Seyed Mehdi Shojaee
In the Twinkling of an Eye, by Seyed Mehdi Shojaee
The Water Urn, by Houshang Moradi Kermani
A Sweet Jam, by Houshang Moradi Kermani

Journal of a Love, Narrative Poetry by Afshin Yadollahi

The Little Goldfish, with Audio CD Narration by Katayoun Riahi

Mullah Nasreddin, illustrated by Alireza Golduzian

The Paper Boat, written and illustrated by Anahita Taymourian

The Circus Outside the Window, written and illustrated by Anahita Taymourian

Sleep Full of Sheep, written and illustrated by Pejman Rahimizadeh

Stillness in a Storm, Collection of Poetry in Persian and English with Audio CD by Saeid Ramezani

47288163R00070

Made in the USA
Charleston, SC
07 October 2015